FIRE BRANDS

FIRE BRANDS

Originally published in *Short Stories*, January 10, 1925.

Published by Wildside Press LLC
wildsidepress.com

CHAPTER I

"I'LL KILL HIM, IF it's the last thing I ever do!" yelped "Sad" Sontag. "I tell yuh, I'm goin' to kill him!"

"Quit it, I tell yuh!" wailed the bartender. "Don't do that!"

Swish! Crash!

"Aw-w-w-w, you danged fool!" The bartender's voice was raised in a wailing crescendo. "Look what yuh went and done."

Sad Sontag's face came up from behind the bar and he looked around solemnly. His serious gray eyes considered the redfaced bartender, shifted to "Swede" Harrigan, his partner, and then considered other occupants of the saloon, who were interested.

"Your darned heels knocked some of my glasses down," complained the bartender. "I told yuh not to do it, didn't I? Didn't I tell yuh not to git up on my bar like that?"

"Uh-huh," nodded Sad. "I s'pose yuh did mention it."

"Mention, hell!" The bartender appealed to the crowd. "I'll leave to any of you."

"You kinda overreached yourself, cowboy," observed Swede.

"Uh-huh," Sad squinted around, felt the back of his neck and shrugged his thin shoulders.

"Well, I s'pose I missed him," he said ruefully, coming from behind the bar. "That's the first darned horsefly that ever bit me from behind and got away with it."

"Gittin' up on my bar and tryin' to hit a fly with a hat!" The bartender was justly indignant. "Where in hell do you fellers think this place is, anyway? Balancin' on your knees on top of my bar and——"

"Wait a minute," interrupted Sad. "If you think that anybody is intensely interested in yore recital, hire a hall. I'll betcha you've got a silv'ry voice, and all that, but not when yo're mad. Right now yuh kinda creak yore words."

"I've got a right to kick, ain't I?"

Sad leaned against the bar, his old sombrero pulled down over his left eye, his shirt collar hiked up around his ears, and squinted reflectively at the irate bartender.

"All right," he nodded. "Go ahead. But, brother, let not yore oration become personal. Use all the 'I's' yuh want to, but keep from sayin' 'you' as much as possible. Proceed."

But the bartender's vocabulary seemed to have oozed away; so he contented himself with picking up what few glasses Sad's heels had smashed when he fell off the bar in his efforts to swat a horsefly.

Sad Sontag was as lean as a grayhound, bronzed as an Indian. His hair was sort of a washed-out sandy color, with one long lock extending down his forehead and joining one of his arched eyebrows, which gave him an habitual astonished expression.

Sad's shirt was of neutral shade; the color having long since faded from the sun and strong soap, his chaps worn and scarred, and his boot heels badly run over on the outer edges, which proved that Sad was bow-legged.

His cartridge belt was of extra width, molded by use to fit the curve of his hip and thigh, and from a scarred holster protruded the plain, black wood butt of a heavy Colt revolver.

Swede Harrigan, his partner, was a composite of Gaelic and Norse; a six foot six inch blond cowboy, with an Irish mouth and nose. His eyes were round and very blue; patient-looking eyes, which belied the nose and mouth below them. His raiment was on a par with that worn by Sad, except that his boot heels were slightly run over on the inner side, which proved that Swede was a little knock-kneed in spite of the fact that he had spent most of his life in a saddle.

They were a nondescript pair, these two cowpunchers; neither handsome nor gaudy. An experienced cattleman would probably pick them out of a crowd as being tophand cowboys; but as far as appearances went they were merely two ordinary cowhands, no better nor worse than the average run.

Nor were they, except that they were joint owners of the TJ cattle outfit in the Sundown country, a hundred miles north of this town of Oreana. Oreana City, they called it, a cow town of a hundred and fifty inhabitants, and the county seat of Pipestone County.

The bartender cooled down considerably when he found that the damage was small, and offered to set up the drinks.

"Gimme a see-gar," said Sad seriously.

"I'll burn m' tongue, too," nodded Swede.

The bartender dug beneath the bar top and drew out a cigar box, which he dusted off and opened.

"Them," he said, tipping the box for a better view, "them is what I call cigars. They costs me three dollars per hundred. Ain't much call for cigars here."

"Hadn't ort to be," agreed Swede. "Prob'ly be less after this."

"It don't do no good to wet 'em that-away," declared the bartender. "I've done it a lot of times, but they won't stick."

Sad's cigar slipped from his fingers onto the floor, while Swede stumbled and broke his against the bar.

"I'll buy a drink of liquor," declared Sad, and added meaningly, "I hope yuh didn't try to make that stick."

"Aw-w-w-w, I didn't mean them cigars," protested the bartender. "I meant that I'd tried it with the ones I smoked."

"Yuh shore get lucid too late," said Swede sadly. "I never did see a bartender that wasn't about forty minutes late."

"Yeah? Well, I wasn't always a bartender."

"Yore work shows it," grinned Sad. "Well, here's how."

Swede grimaced and coughed.

"My gosh!" he gasped. "That's the first time I ever made a test-tube out of my insides. Hooh! I'll betcha that inside of fifteen minutes there won't be nothin' left of me except my ring and the case of my watch. Nitric acid!"

"Twenty years in the wood," declared the bartender.

"Ah-h-h-h-h!" Sad clung to the bar, gasping like a drowning man, his eyes closed painfully. The bartender had not yet taken his drink, and now he slid it beneath the bar and dumped it into the slacktub, where he washed his glasses.

He sniffed at the bottles. It seemed to smell all right.

"It seems to be all right," he said.

"Yeah, it's all right, but it's got kind of a whisky taste," said Sad.

"My gosh, it is whisky!"

"It is?" Sad's eyebrows lifted incredulously. "Do you mean to tell me—ah, no, it cannot be!"

"He says it straight enough," said Swede seriously. He and Sad stared at each other wonderingly, turned together, stared at the bartender and went slowly out into the street; while the bartender rubbed his chin and wondered what on earth it was all about anyway.

Sad and Swede walked up the narrow sidewalk, their faces very solemn until they looked at each other and burst into laughter.

"Now that poor bartender'll wonder whether we're crazy or he is," chuckled Sad. "Didja see him ditch his drink, Swede?"

"Did I? Ha, ha, ha, ha! It's got a whisky taste!" Swede went into paroxisms of unholy glee.

They stopped near the entrance of a hall which led up to the county offices, and began perusing the assorted notices tacked to the wall. Sad seemed interested in one particular notice which concerned a sheriff's sale.

"What day is this, Swede?" he asked.

"This is Monday, the seventh of August."

"Thasso? Huh! Say, when did that feller tell us that this here sale was to be pulled off?"

"On the ninth."

"Well, he lied several days," complained Sad. "Here's the notice, which says it'll be pulled off on the twelfth."

Swede moved over and squinted at the notice, which declared that on the twelfth day of August the sheriff of Pipestone county would sell at public auction everything belonging to the Bar S ranch. The sheriff had even gone to the trouble of drawing a pen design of the brand, which was a letter S, with a straight bar over the top.

"I reckon some of these Oreana folks can't read; so he has to draw a pitcher of it," grinned Swede. "Dang it, that makes it kinda bad for us, Sad. What'll we do?"

Sad scratched his head and squinted dismally.

"I dunno. I don't care to hive up in this place for very long, but we came here to see what we could buy at that sale; so we might as well stay here and see it through. What do yuh think?"

"I don't care. It's all right with me, if we can find somethin' to do around this town."

"All right, we'll stay, Swede. The first thing we better do is to put them broncs in a stable and find us a place to stay."

As they turned away from the bulletin board a yellow dog shot around the corner, yelping as only a yellow dog can yelp, while behind it, tied securely to its tail, bounded a tin can.

For a fraction of a second the yellow dog hesitated as it turned the corner, and then it headed straight for Sad and Swede. The word "headed" is hardly descriptive of its speed. Afterward Swede swore that something drew a yellow streak from his feet to the corner, and then rubbed it out.

At any rate, the dog, running blindly, attempted to go between Swede's legs, which were slightly knock-kneed, and Swede flipped upside down, while the tin can whipped around his ankle, snapping the twine cord, and the yellow dog streaked away up the street, leaving Swede on his hands and knees, swearing just enough.

Immediately following the dog came a boy of about twelve, his freckled face streaked with dusty tears, his rusty hair rumpled belligerently. He stopped and looked at Swede, who was untangling the cord from around his boot. Sad grinned at the youngster, who came closer, crooking his neck to look past them.

"Where'd Boze go?" he drawled.

"Was that Boze?" asked Sad.

"Yeah." The kid scratched one of his bare feet and looked back.

"Yuh hadn't ort to tie cans on yore dog," said Swede.

"Aw-w-w, hell!" The youngster spat dryly and hitched up his ragged overalls. "I never done it. It was some of them dad-durned square-heads from the Box 8. By grab, if I ever git big enough I'll shore tie off to one of them pelicans and yank real hard."

"Aw, shucks!" Sad grew sympathetic. "Somebody pickin' on yuh, Bud?"

"Yeah—but my name ain't Bud. I'm Percival Cadwallader Steeb. Mostly everybody calls me 'Speck' Steeb. And," Speck sighed dismally and wiped his cheeks, "I ain't havin' good luck."

"Ain't yuh, Speck?" queried Swede.

"Nope. Me and Boze ran away from that derned Box 8 outfit."

"Are you livin' there, or jist punchin' cows for 'em?" asked Sad.

"Aw, I ain't big enough to be a 'hand' yet. They thought I was livin' there, but I ain't. And by the busted tail of a longhorn steer, I ain't goin' to live there neither. I'm through."

"A feller like you ort to pick and choose," nodded Swede.

An old man drove up and got out of his wagon in front of a store. His equipage consisted of a rickety buckboard and a pair of mismated horses. He was little short of seventy years of age, with a long, white beard and white hair. His face was seamed deeply and colored like an old parchment, which only accentuated the white of his beard and hair.

Three cowpunchers rounded the corner beyond the store and went inside, while the old man followed them in. Speck scowled at the three punchers.

"Them punchers is the jiggers from the Box 8 that tin canned Boze," he informed them. "Took all three of 'em to hawg-tie me, y'betcha. That old man in the wagon is Eph Wyatt. He c'n whip his weight in anythin' yuh want to mention."

"Pretty old to be fightin', ain't he?" ventured Sad.

"Well, I dunno. Paw said that old Eph got fightener every year."

Sad laughed and patted the youngster on the shoulder.

"Some folks are that way, Speck," he said. "Where is yore father?"

Speck's eyes suddenly filled with tears and he shoved both hands down deep in his pockets.

Sad and Swede exchanged a quick glance, as Speck looked up at them and said, "Well, yuh see, he—he's dead now."

"Aw, gosh!" exploded Sad mournfully. "Yuh see, Speck, we didn't know about that."

"Thasall right," Speck smiled through his tears. "Folks never learn nothin' unless they ask questions. My dad owned the Bar S ranch."

"Oh, yeah," Sad nodded thoughtfully. "Well, ain't yuh got no relations, Speck? Nobody to look after yuh?"

"No-o-o," Speck sighed deeply. "Anyway, I dunno any. Pa wasn't much fer relations. Lot of these folks around here got to tryin' to figure out what to do with me, and I'll betcha some of 'em won't git the cramps out of their brains for a year.

"Bill Wyatt says he can use a boy about my size out at the Box 8; so they sends me out there. Bill's that old man's nephew, but he's owner of the Box 8. I stayed two days, and I'll tell a man I worked. Whooee! Bill hates Boze. Bill hates everythin', I reckon. Anyway, he run Boze off the ranch twice, but Boze comes back every time. Then Bill tells me to run the dog off the ranch and keep him off; so I run Boze plumb down here where," Speck grinned wisely, "where I can keep us both off."

"And then they come down here and tin can the dog, eh?" said Swede.

"Shore did. But Boze'll come back."

"That part's all right, but what about you?" asked Sad.

"Don't nobody need to worry about me," assured Speck.

"Uh-huh," Sad scratched his head thoughtfully. He admired the independent attitude of the youngster.

"I'll git along," remarked Speck. "All I ask is that they leave me and Boze alone. There's the little son-of-a-gun now."

Boze had ventured back to the corner beyond the store, and was peering around into the street. Speck whistled to the dog, which ran to meet him. Sad and Swede grinned at each other and walked to the store entrance, while the boy and dog romped farther up the street.

"Somebody's hot under the collar," observed Swede, as sounds of an argument from within the store greeted their entrance.

"I tell yuh, I don't want him around!" It was Bill Wyatt, a thin-faced, buck-toothed cowboy, speaking. He rowled his spurs savagely against the counter and spat accurately at a sawdust-filled box.

"That's all right."

This remark came ponderously from Al Weller, the big storekeeper.

"It was your own idea, Bill."

"Yeah, that's right," nodded Bill. "But I thought he'd be worth somethin'. Hell, he won't work!"

Old Eph Wyatt turned his head and squinted at his nephew.

"You wasn't payin' him no wages, was yuh, Bill?"

"Not so yuh could notice it."

"I didn't think yuh was, Bill. Yuh can hire men for forty a month, and yuh might stop long enough to remember that the kid ain't more'n twelve years old."

"I was givin' him a home," retorted Bill.

"You wasn't givin him nothin'—he had to earn one."

"There's no use quarrelin'," said the storekeeper quickly.

"I'm not quarrelin'," said the old man. "The poor kid got a tough deal all the way around. I liked Jim Steeb. He was a damn fool to drink himself to death, lose everythin' and throw the kid into a community that's got more kids than they know what to do with.

"Bill had an idea that he could git some cheap labor, I reckon. No, I ain't sayin' that a little work will hurt any kid, but a youngster like him hadn't ort to have to work twelve hours per day for his bed and three meals."

"I dunno yet jist why yo're hornin' into this," declared Bill.

His uncle squinted at Bill closely; so intently that the younger man shifted uneasily.

"You didn't think that I cared to explain, did yuh?" asked the old man slowly. "I ain't never been in the habit to apologizin' for hornin' into an argument, have I?"

"Thasall right, Eph." The storekeeper was a trifle anxious.

"Well, I don't care what yuh do." Bill shrugged his shoulders and threw some silver on the counter.

"Gimme some smokin' and papers, Al."

As he pocketed the desired articles, Speck and Boze came in. The dog slouched at the boy's heels, recognizing its enemies, but Speck was unafraid. All conversation ceased, as the boy and dog came up to the group. Some of the men had noticed Sad and Swede, but the argument had been too interesting for them to pay much attention to a pair of strange cowboys.

"That dog don't know when to git insulted," laughed Bill.

"You let that dog alone," said Speck firmly. "He ain't never done nothin' to you, Bill Wyatt."

Bill laughed at Speck and started for Boze, who darted back toward the door, barking snappily.

"You let that dog alone!" shrilled Speck, blocking Bill. "By golly, some day I'll be big enough——"

But Speck's prophecy was not finished when Bill's open palm splatted against his ear, sending him sideways into the counter, and Bill started toward the frightened dog.

"You hadn't ought to do that." Sad Sontag stepped around the end of a display table between Bill and the dog. There was no threat in Sad's voice nor actions. He was smiling with his mouth, but his eyes were serious.

"Hadn't, eh?" Bill stopped and looked Sad over curiously. It was the first time he had ever seen this strange cowpuncher. Then he turned his head and looked at Swede, who was lounging easily against a counter, paying no attention to what Sad was doing, because his entire attention centered on the two men who had come in with Bill Wyatt.

Bill's eyes came back to Sad.

"What's the idea of you hornin' into this?" he demanded.

"I ain't hornin' in," smiled Sad. "I was just tellin' yuh."

Boze seemed to realize that the immediate danger was over, so he came over and sniffed at Sad's boots. Speck had regained his feet, and was busily rubbing a very red ear. Bill looked back at his two men and found them centering their attention on Swede.

"And," said Sad softly, "any man that would slap kids and tie cans on a pup's tail is a low bred coyote."

The storekeeper ducked low behind the counter, and the old man edged slowly out of line with the two men. They knew that Bill Wyatt was deadly with a six-shooter, and that there could be but one answer to that insult.

Still Bill Wyatt did not move. His half-closed eyes looked into the wide open gray ones of Sad Sontag, which seemed to hypnotize him. Neither of them had made any motion toward a gun.

"A feller that would hit a kid ain't got the guts to fight." Sad's voice was pitched low, but carried clearly. "You might fight, if yuh was in a corner—but I doubt it."

But Bill Wyatt did not move. Sad inched toward him, coming closer and closer. One of Bill's men swore softly, wonderingly. They could not see Bill's face.

Suddenly Sad's left hand shot out, grasped the brim of Bill's sombrero and yanked it down over Bill's eyes. It was done so quickly that Bill did not have time to jerk away, and he stumbled forward from the pull.

But the hypnotic spell was broken. Bill ripped out a foul oath, as he flung back the hat and flipped out his gun; but the barrel of Sad's struck him across the right wrist, forcing him to drop his gun, and the next instant he measured his full length under the table from a left swing which caught him full in the ear.

"Glory to gosh!" whooped Speck. "Right in the ear!"

Bill's two men had not moved during the fight, for the simple reason that the blond-headed Swede still leaned against the counter, dangling a big six-shooter in his right hand; his lips puckered in a whistle, while his round blue eyes never wavered.

Sad kicked Bill's gun aside and waited for him to get up; but Bill was in no great hurry. He slid from under the table, rubbing his swelling ear and seemed inclined to wonder what it was all about.

"You know now how it feels to get hit in the ear, don'tcha?" chuckled Speck. "Mebbe next time you'll have a little sense."

Bill got slowly to his feet and walked out of the store, while Abe Snow and "Snipe" Lee, his two men, followed him out. They gave Swede a wide berth in passing.

"And thus endeth that chapter," smiled Sad.

"Mebbe not," said old Eph Wyatt dubiously. "My nephew Bill won't forget it for a mighty long time, stranger."

"Memories has caused a lot of folks to lose their minds," grinned Sad, rumpling Speck's hair and feeling of his ear.

"Aw, it don't hurt now," protested Speck. "The wallop you gave Bill Wyatt cured me. Whooee, I'll betcha he's sore!"

A man was coming into the store, but turned to look across at the hitchrack, where the three men from the Box 8 were mounting. It was Buck Rainey, the sheriff, a short, heavy-set individual, with a yellow mustache and squinty eyes.

He came on in, glanced casually at Sad and Swede and spoke to the others.

"You missed a circus, Buck," said Eph Wyatt, whose feelings in regard to his nephew were well known. "Bill jist got knocked cold."

"Yeah?" The sheriff elevated his eyebrows. "How come, Eph?"

The old man laughed and detailed the story, while the sheriff stroked his mustache and considered Sad and Swede.

"And he popped him right in the ear," added Speck jubilantly.

"Uh-huh." The sheriff scratched his nose thoughtfully. "It's a wonder that Bill didn't start shootin'."

"It's got me beat," said the storekeeper. "He jist stood and took it. I don't sabe Bill."

"Is he supposed to be a bad man?" asked Sad.

"Well," drawled the sheriff, "a feller don't have to be so awful darned bad to reach for a gun at a time like that."

"I don't think he's got brains enough to know when he's been insulted," laughed Swede.

"Mebbe not," the sheriff grinned. "But Bill is usually the one to start trouble."

"Mebbe I packed it to him too fast," grinned Sad. "You're the sheriff, ain't yuh?"

"Yeah."

"I'm Sontag. My pardner's name is Harrigan. We own a ranch in the Sundown country, and we're down here to see what we can buy at that Bar S sale."

"Oh, yeah. Pleased to meetcha. Bar S sale, eh? Uh-hu-u-uh. What didja figure on buyin'?"

"Mebbe a few head of stock. We heard that there was quite a bunch of cattle and horses."

"Yeah? Well, it won't be held until the twelfth."

"That's all right. We got some wrong information and come down too soon."

The sheriff turned to Eph Wyatt and the storekeeper.

"I've been wonderin' what we're goin' to do with this kid." He pointed at Speck, who was perched on a counter. "Bill said he'd take care of him, but that's all off now, I suppose. Makes it bad for the kid."

"I wish you'd quit worryin' about me," said Speck. "I ain't askin' for nothin' but a job. I c'n work my way along."

"You ain't big enough to work," declared the sheriff. "Your place is in school."

"How'd yuh like to work for me?" asked the old man.

"Huh! I dunno," Speck wriggled his toes. "Me and you'd prob'ly get along fine, Mr. Wyatt. Dad said you was the fightenest son-of-a-gun he ever seen—and I like to fight, too."

The old man laughed softly and walked over to Speck.

"Fightin' don't git yuh much, Speck. I'm all alone on that old ranch out there, and I sure need somebody to help me. Suppose yuh come out and live with me."

"Well—" Speck hesitated. "Well, I'll do it."

"He ain't big enough to do much work," said the sheriff.

"No, and he won't have much to do." Eph Wyatt turned to the sheriff. "I'll take him out there with me jist the same. If me and him gits along all right. I'll—I'll adopt him accordin' to law."

"You'll adopt him?"

"I shore will. Ain't no law ag'in it, is there, Buck?"

"Sure ain't, Eph."

"What does adoptin' mean?" asked Speck.

"Takin' out papers to make yuh the same as my son," explained the old man.

"Yea-a-a-ah?" Speck's eyes widened. "What about Boze?"

"Well, he comes along," laughed the old man. "We won't need no papers for the pup. C'mon."

The old man started for the door, with the boy and the pup close behind him. At the doorway Speck turned and came back to Sad, holding out his hand.

"Much obliged, Mr. Sontag," he said. "Hope to meetcha ag'in."

"Yo're shore welcome, Speck," laughed Sad as they shook hands. "I hope yore luck has turned."

"She's beginnin' to bend a little," grinned Speck. "S'long."

They watched Speck climb up on the seat beside the old man, while Boze danced around in the rear of the buckboard and barked his approval of the equipage.

"Well, I hope it works out all right," said the sheriff. "It sure was hard to find out what to do with that kid."

"What killed his father?" asked Swede.

"Liquor. He spent most of his time at the Oreana saloon. It was too danged bad. Jim Steeb wasn't a bad sort of a feller. His wife died a year ago, and it kinda ruined him. This ain't exactly a sheriff's sale. Yuh see, 'Bunty' O'Neil, who owns the Oreana saloon, has enough of Steeb's notes to probably cover everythin' on the Bar S."

"Steeb just drank up his ranch, eh?" queried Sad.

"Uh-huh. There may be a little over, after O'Neil gets paid, but I doubt it. I've got three men in the hills now, roundin' up the Bar S stock."

"What sort of a person is Bill Wyatt?"

"Bill Wyatt? Well, he's all right, I reckon. Bill's kinda touchy, and ain't noways honey-flavored, yuh know. He owns the Box 8 outfit and runs quite a lot of stock. That old Eph Wyatt is his uncle. Old Eph is a cantankerous old reptile, but he's good-hearted. I dunno how him and the kid will hit it off together."

"Is Bill Wyatt married?"

"Naw."

"Owned the Box 8 very long?"

"Couple of years."

"Buy out a brand, or register his own?"

"Registered his own. Used to be the 8 outfit; so he changed it to the Box 8. Say, what's the idea of all these questions?"

"Curiosity, thasall, Sheriff," laughed Sad. "Nice weather we're havin'."

"Uh-hu-u-uh." The sheriff walked down the street toward his office, where three men were dismounting, while Sad and Swede went in the opposite direction, looking for a place to call home for a few days.

CHAPTER II

BUNTY O'NEIL OF THE Oreana saloon was not what you would call a lovable character. He was of medium height, thick of neck and broad of shoulder. His face was blocky, expressionless, swarthy; a hard-headed individual, whose bunting practice in a fight had given him his nickname. He would grasp an opponent with his huge hands, yank him forward and butt him with his head. Only in rare cases did Bunty fail to put his opponent *hors de combat*. It was an unlooked for move, except where Bunty's system was well known.

Bunty had once worked it successfully on Bill Wyatt. Bill had wakened up about fifteen minutes later and found that both of his eyes were of a purple tint and did not admit much light. He had waited for the swelling to go down, had walked up behind Bunty in the Oreana saloon and crowned him with the barrel of a six-shooter.

Bunty had had six stitches taken in his scalp, and had sent word to Bill Wyatt to keep out of the Oreana. Bill did. This had happened six months prior to Sad and Swede's coming to Oreana, but Bill had never been in the place since. Yet Bill had known Bunty in the northern part of the state, and it was Bill who had induced Bunty to come to Oreana and buy out the Oreana saloon and gambling house.

Just now Bunty and the sheriff were standing on the porch of the saloon, talking seriously. It was the day after Sad and Swede had come to Oreana.

"You say they brought in three hundred and ten head?" asked Bunty. The sheriff nodded.

"Yeah. They're in the old pasture at the Bar S. The boys have gone down into the lower ranges now, but they won't be able to round up everythin' for a couple days. There's enough feed in the pasture for a few days."

"That's good." Bunty smiled contentedly. "Three hundred and ten head, eh? Mebbe I'll get my money after all, Buck."

"I reckon yuh will, Bunty. For gosh sake, how much money did Jim Steeb owe yuh, anyway?"

Bunty grinned widely and shook his head.

"Jim plunged quite a lot, Buck. His whisky bill ain't more than a few hundred, but his faro and poker playin' sure cost money. I reckon the notes he gave me will come close to ten thousand."

The sheriff whistled his amazement.

"As much as that, Bunty? Huh! Yuh know," the sheriff squinted thoughtfully. "Yuh know, it seems too darned bad Jim went through all that money and didn't leave a darned thing for the kid. Old Eph Wyatt is goin' to adopt him, I think."

"Old Eph?" Bunty laughed. "Goin' to adopt him, eh? Well, well!"

Just then Sad and Swede came out of the hotel and sauntered toward the general store.

"They tell me that one of them fellers took a fall out of Bill Wyatt," said Bunty thoughtfully.

"The skinny one. They're down here to buy some stock at the sale. The skinny one's name is Sontag and the other is Harrigan. Seem like a salty pair of fellers. Sontag tells me that they own a ranch in the Sundown country."

"Well, all I care about it is to get my money out of the deal, Buck."

They went into the saloon, as Sad and Swede crossed the street, following them inside. The sheriff greeted them warmly and introduced them to Bunty as the owner of the Oreana. There was little activity in the place and the day was warm.

"You interested in the Bar S sale?" asked Bunty.

Sad nodded. "Kinda. We're lookin' for some stock, and thought this might be a chance to buy some reasonable. Course we don't want a lot of runts."

"We might take a ride out to the Bar S this evenin'," suggested the sheriff. "The boys threw three hundred and ten head into the pasture last night, and it might help yuh some to look 'em over."

"We'd sure appreciate the chance," agreed Sad.

They spent the rest of the day, loafing in the shade, and did not start for the Bar S until late in the afternoon. It was five miles to the ranch, located northeast of Oreana. The ranch buildings were badly in need of repair, but it was easy to see that at one time the Bar S had been considerable of a ranch.

There was no one at the place, and the sheriff explained that there had been no one in charge since the death of Steeb. They rode out past the corrals and on to a knoll that furnished a view of the Bar S pasture, which contained about a hundred acres.

But there were no cattle in sight. The sheriff gnawed his mustache and squinted around wonderingly.

"'S funny," he muttered. "They were here last night."

"Are yuh sure this is the place?" asked Swede.

"Am I sure? I'm jist as sure as anythin'," replied the sheriff and spurred his horse off the knoll.

They rode to the lower end of the pasture, and it did not take them long to find where the barb-wires had been cut, and about a hundred feet of them ripped off the posts.

"They knowed how to do it," observed Sad. "They cut the wires, bunched the ends, tied 'em to a rope and jist rode 'em loose."

"And let the whole herd drift," observed the sheriff. "Well, that's jist plumb meanness, I'd say."

Sad looked at the sheriff and grinned softly.

"Sheriff, do you think that they just turned them cows loose?"

"Eh?" The sheriff's eyebrows lifted slightly. "Yuh don't think that anybody would try to rustle a herd like that, do yuh?"

"Why not?"

"Well, I dunno. Yuh can't git away with that many. Anybody would be a fool to try and steal a herd like that."

"All right," Sad grinned widely and turned his horse. "You know the morals of this country better than we do."

They rode back to Oreana and stabled their horses. The sheriff was very thoughtful during the ride, but could hardly bring himself to believe that anyone would try and steal three hundred and ten head of cattle in one herd.

"I think that someone is jist doin' it to be mean," he declared.

"And I think they're doin' it for profit," laughed Sad.

It did not take the sheriff long to impart the story to Bunty O'Neil, who swore under his breath and questioned them closely. The sheriff told Bunty what he thought about it, but Bunty did not agree.

"They've had about twenty-four hours start," observed Bunty. "And yuh can move a big herd a long ways in that length of time. It's so dry in the hills that yuh couldn't trail a herd; so the best yuh can do is to trust to luck."

"It kinda looks like we might as well go home," observed Swede. "No use of us stayin' here, if there ain't no cows for sale."

Bunty's eyes grew hard as he leaned on the bar and toyed with his glass. The sheriff cleared his throat and sent his glass spinning down the bar.

"Bunty has got a lot of notes against the Bar S," he explained. "And if there ain't no cows—Bunty loses."

"That's the how of it, eh?" said Sad.

"Yeah, that's the how of it," said Bunty angrily. "And I'll get them cows—or get somethin'."

"You've got sort of an idea who took 'em, ain't yuh?" asked Sad.

"How would I?" snapped Bunty.

"I dunno how yuh would—I'm no mindreader," and Sad walked away from the bar and grew interested in a poker game.

Bunty looked after him, an angry glint in his eyes, but said nothing until Swede walked away.

"What did he mean, Buck?" he then asked.

The sheriff shook his head. "I dunno. I hope the boys show up tomorrow, but I'm scared they won't. We've got to try and find them missin' cattle, that's a cinch. I don't believe yet that anybody had the nerve to try and steal a herd that big."

The sheriff left the saloon, but Bunty remained at the bar, drinking his own liquor. It was not often that Bunty drank heavily. Liquor made him quarrelsome. Several patrons steered clear of the bar and had their drinks served at a table, when they realized that Bunty was on a spree.

Bunty leaned across the bar and motioned the bartender closer.

"What did that skinny puncher mean?" he demanded.

"The skinny one? I dunno what he said, Bunty. Personally, I think he's crazy. The damn fool fell off the bar yesterday, tryin' to hit a horsefly with his hat. And they said that there was whisky in the drinks we served here. What are they—e-vangelists?"

Bunty grunted an oath and reached for the bottle. Sad and Swede were coming toward the bar, heading for the door. Bunty stepped in front of Sad and motioned them to stop and drink with him.

"Yuh ain't in no hurry, are yuh?" he growled.

"Not a bit," grinned Sad.

"I'm glad yuh ain't—'cause you'd stop anyway."

Sad glanced keenly at Bunty. He realized that the other was angry over something, and that he might be a hard man to handle.

"I'm not buyin' yuh any drinks," Bunty informed them harshly. "I only buy drinks for my friends."

"Then have a drink on me," grinned Sad.

"No, I won't do that, either." Bunty moved in closer to Sad.

"I want to know what wuh mean by that remark a while ago—about yuh not bein' a mind reader."

"Oh!" Sad squinted thoughtfully. "Well, I'm not, Bunty. I'll leave it to Swede if I am."

"You'll leave nothin' to nobody! C'mere!"

Bunty grasped Sad by the shoulders, sinking his powerful fingers deeply into the flesh. It was the prelude to crashing the top of his head into Sad's face—and Sad realized it.

But Bunty did not work fast enough. With a sudden shift of his feet, Sad kicked Bunty in the shins so hard that the hotelman forgot everything except the excruciating pain. His hands jerked loose and he reached for his shins just in time to get Sad's fist square in his nose, with the full swinging weight of the wiry cowpuncher behind it.

The blow straightened Bunty back onto his heels, and before he could catch his balance Sad was into him, smashing with both hands to the head, and Bunty went reeling across the room to crash into the back of a poker player's chair and go flat on his back.

At least a dozen men had seen the whole affair. They had expected Bunty to butt the face almost off this thin cowpuncher and end the fight to suit himself. But they had reckoned without Sad Sontag, who now was standing against the bar, blowing on his sore knuckles and grinning widely.

There was little commotion. A couple of men picked Bunty up and half-dragged him to the rear of the room, where they could wash him off, the poker player adjusted his chair and the games went on.

Sad and Swede went back to the hotel, where Sad procured some hot water in which to bathe his swollen right hand. Swede became pessimistic.

"Aw, let's go home," he argued dismally. "You've whipped both of their best fighters. This here town kinda palls upon me, Sad, and I'd crave to ride home."

"I've had a pretty fair time," said Sad seriously, examining his knuckles. "I s'pose Bunty was aimin' to butt me in the face, wasn't he?"

"That's his style," agreed Swede wearily. "There ain't no cows to be bought; so we might as well start home t'morrow."

"It's a funny thing about them stolen cows," observed Sad, as he stretched out on the bed and began rolling a cigarette. "I'll betcha anythin' that Bunty knows who stole 'em. Somebody knows that Bunty has notes against the Bar S; so they crimped his chances to collect by stealin' the whole danged herd.

"There's somebody who hates Bunty quite a lot, Swede. It ain't no little job to steal three hundred head of cattle. Mebbe they just done it to aggravate the sheriff, or Bunty."

"Then yuh think they'll have enough stock for us to wait for the sale?"

"Yuh never can tell." Sad blew smoke rings at the dingy ceiling. "I've got a hunch that they won't. Tomorrow we'll find out more about it, and if it don't look more promisin' we'll rattle our hocks out of Oreana. I've had all the fightin' I want, y'betcha."

"We might ride out past old Eph Wyatt's place," suggester Swede. "I'm kinda curious to know how the old man and the kid are comin' along."

"Yeah, we'll do that, Swede. I'm curious about that kid myself. Somehow I've got a hunch that the kid ain't had a square deal."

"Just how do yuh mean, Sad?"

"Aw, just kinda mind readin', I reckon."

CHAPTER III

IT WAS THE FOLLOWING morning at Eph Wyatt's ranch-house that Speck Steeb, the freckle-faced boy, leaned against the doorway and rubbed a sore jaw. Sitting on the edge of the step was old Eph Wyatt, busily engaged in cleaning a Winchester rifle; while the dog, Boze, chased a rooster across the yard, his mouth filled with feathers.

The old man stuffed cartridges into the loading gate, levered a shell into the chamber of the rifle and handed it to Speck, who took it gingerly and squatted down on the step.

"Pull a little finer, son," advised the old man. "Them last two shots went six inches high."

Speck cuddled the stock against his shoulder, resting the heavy barrel between his knees. The old man's eyes squinted closely at Speck's trigger finger, which tightened slowly, surely; and the big caliber rifle shook Speck from head to heels.

From down back of the stable, a tin can flipped off a corral post and went spinning into the brush. Speck blinked painfully, but a grin wreathed his lips, when he noted that the can was not on the post.

"Pretty good!" chuckled the old man. "Pretty good!"

"Pretty good, hell!" snorted Speck indignantly. "That's perfect."

"Yeah, I'll betcha it is," agreed the old man. "Any old time a little kid can hit a tin can at a hundred yards with a 45-90, it's jist a little better than perfect. How's the shoulder?"

"Jist' like a blamed boil. Geemighty, I never knowed a rifle could kick that-away."

"And yuh squeezed the trigger, too," applauded the old man. "Yuh knowed it was goin' to kick, but yuh had the nerve to pull slow. Speck, me and you are goin' to git along, y'betcha. Well, that ends the first lesson."

The old man put the gun in the house and came back to the porch.

"We're goin' to town," he decided. "We'll hook onto a lawyer feller and have him fix up the papers—if yuh don't mind, Speck."

Speck rubbed his shoulder reflectively.

"Yuh mean the papers that make me your son?"

"Yeah."

Speck squinted up at the old man thoughtfully.

"Why are yuh doin' this, Mr. Wyatt? I ain't nothin' to you."

"Why?" The old man looked out across the hills, shading his eyes from the sun. "Well, mebbe it's 'cause I kinda like yuh, son. I'm gittin' old, I s'pose. And livin' alone don't make yuh stay young. I ain't got no livin' relation, except Bill Wyatt, and," he hesitated for a moment before he looked down at Speck, "I've allus been quite a hand for relatives."

"And that's all the reasons yuh got, Mr. Wyatt?"

"Well, that's all I care to speak about."

"Uh-huh." Speck bobbed his head wisely. "Well, I can stand it, if you can." He got to his feet and held out his hand. "Shake, pardner."

They shook hands gravely. It was a solemn pact between two old men; two of the fightenest sons-of-guns in the Oreana country.

They went to the stable, harnessed the mismated horses to the old buckboard and drove up to the house, where the old man got the rifle and leaned it against the seat between them.

As they drove away the old man looked back at the house and said, "Speck, I reckon we'll have to fix up the old place a little now. I've kinda let her drift for the last few years 'cause there wasn't no object in havin' it handled right. I've got a right smart of cows in them hills. It ain't took much for my keep. When I needed money I'd sell a handful of critters.

"This here Diamond W has got the best water-holes in this country, and it shore could be made into a fine ranch. The old house needs fixin' a lot, and the barn's swaybacked. Some day a wind will come along and blow the corral away, I s'pose. But we'll fix her all up now."

The old man chuckled and slapped Speck on the back.

"By golly, son, we'll show 'em, eh?"

"Danged right," nodded Speck.

They drove down through a brushy swale and around the point of a ridge, where a long line of cottonwoods angled up through a narrow canyon. The road was rutty and the horses were traveling at a slow walk, when the larger of the two beasts lurched sideways and went down in a tangle.

Almost at the same moment the report of a rifle broke the stillness. The other horse reared wildly, swung over the body of its mate and fell back against the buckboard, squealing and kicking. The shock of it all caused Speck to stand up, clinging to the back of the seat, and the next moment he was picked up by the old man and hurled bodily into a clump of brush beside the road.

And while Speck was still in the air the old man grasped the rifle and started to jump, but a bullet shocked him heavily and he went down sideways, falling just outside the wheels. Boze had jumped from the rear of the buckboard and scuttled into the brush, as though he knew what was taking place.

Speck landed in the brush head-first, but managed to extricate himself quickly and crawl back to the old man, whose hair and beard were already dyed with crimson. Speck's eyes were wide with fright, but his jaw was clenched tightly, as he clawed the rifle from between the wheels and ducked back into the brush.

"Gosh a'mighty!" he panted. "Bushwhacked, by jing!"

He remained quiet long enough to calm his breathing. One horse was dead, the other down in a tangle of harness, unable to get up. Speck rubbed his nose and considered his predicament. From where he squatted he was unable to see anything of the surrounding country, so he crawled back through the brush until he could get on higher ground.

He felt reasonably sure that the shooter had been hidden in that line of cottonwoods, and that they, or he, would try and get a close view of the buckboard to see just what they had accomplished.

Working further up the side of the swale, he found a good spot to wait. It gave him a fairly good view of the surrounding country, although he could not see the buckboard. He could see Boze far down the road, hunting for gophers.

Suddenly he saw two riders emerge from a thicket on the right-hand side of the cottonwoods. They were going cautiously, and it seemed to Speck that they were intent on seeing what was down the road. The brush was horse-high; so he was unable to identify their horses.

They were about three hundred yards away, when Speck raised the sights on his rifle and rested it across a limb. It did not occur to him that he was about to shoot at a human being. They were the ones who had shot his benefactor, and he was going to repay them in kind. He flinched from the pressure of the rifle butt against his sore shoulder, but he gritted his teeth and muttered, "Squeeze, dang yuh—don't yank!"

The big rifle crashed the silence and the black powder fumes drifted back into Speck's wide open mouth. He coughed slightly and dropped lower, his lips grimacing disgustedly.

"Yuh yanked!" he said aloud in self accusation. "Yuh darned fool, yuh yanked. Why didn't yuh squeeze? Yanked, and jerked the sight plumb off to the right."

He could not see the two riders now, but he felt sure that the smoke from his shot had disclosed his hiding place; so he began crawling further up the canyon, going toward where he had seen the two riders.

Speck was wise enough to feel that they would not expect him to come toward them. He gained the cottonwoods and waited. There was not a sound, except the rustling of the trees. Far up the canyon a magpie squawked, sounding almost human.

Speck ducked low and followed the trees, stopping every few yards to listen. Then he left the cottonwoods and made his way around through the brush. He, too, wanted to get a view of what might be down at the buckboard.

Suddenly he stopped short, his mouth open in amazement. He had found the two horses. They had been left in a choke-cherry thicket, almost in the same spot where they had been when Speck shot at the riders. He spoke softly to the horses, worked his way past them, but was unable to get a glimpse of the road.

"Ding dang such luck!" he grumbled. "Feller never knows what will happen next in this Western country." He had heard his father use that expression many times, and it seemed applicable to his present predicament.

"Well," he decided philosophically, "the least I can do is to git help."

He went back to the horses, selected the smaller of the two, a blaze-faced roan, and managed to get into the saddle, but lost his rifle in the attempt. Cautiously he worked the horse back through the brush, swung along the side of the hill for about a quarter of a mile before turning back toward the road.

He managed to get his feet hooked in above the stirrups, which gave him a secure seat in the saddle, and in this manner, with his rusty hair standing almost on end and his skinny elbows beating a tattoo on his ribs, he headed swiftly toward Oreana.

Meanwhile down at the buckboard stood Sad and Swede, looking down at old Eph Wyatt, propped against a wheel. The old man's face and beard were well streaked with gore, which he mopped away with Sad's handkerchief.

"Think it's deep enough to amount to anythin'?" asked Swede.

"Don't hurt much," said the old man. "I feel kinda numb, that's all. By gosh, that shore was a close call, gents. It bumped me so darned hard I never even knowed when it hit."

"Where do yuh reckon the kid went?" queried Sad.

"I dunno. I throwed him into the brush after the team went down."

"Prob'ly high-tailed it for parts unknown," laughed Swede.

"Not that kid." The old man spoke with conviction. "Speck ain't the runnin' kind. And he took the rifle. Say, I don't think I'm hurt much." He got to his feet and clung to the wheel. "Kinda dizzy and m' head aches a little. Gittin' too old to stand many tunks on the head like that."

"Got any idea who shot yuh?" asked Sad.

"Nope."

"Uh-huh," Sad nodded seriously. "We can start by eliminatin' yore friends. Who hates yuh the worst?"

"The worst?" Old Eph squinted painfully. "Well, I dunno. Yuh see, I ain't got no friends; so yuh don't need to eliminate anybody. I wish I knowed where that kid went. If anybody hurts him I'll shore make 'em run fast and jump high."

"You've got two good little assistants, old timer," grinned Sad. "We kinda like Speck, too. Do yuh want to find out who shot yuh?"

"Do I?" The old man laughed wearily. "Yo're danged right I do."

"All right," grinned Sad. "Mebbe we can find out, if we work real fast. Swede, you go and collect the horses."

And while Swede went after the horses Sad untangled the uninjured horse and helped it to its feet. But he did not unhitch it from the buckboard. In a few minutes Swede came back, riding Sad's bay horse, and carrying Eph Wyatt's rifle.

"My bronc was gone," he told them, "and they left this here rifle in its place."

Sad grinned and rubbed his nose violently.

"Looks like the work of a pack-rat, Swede. They always trade somethin'." He turned to the old man. "Speck's all right. He just out-smarted us, thasall, and swiped a horse. We've got to hurry before Oreana descends upon us in a gob, and we've only got one piece of rollin' stock; so you get aboard, old timer."

"Shucks, I can walk," protested the old man.

"Yo're supposed to be dead," grinned Sad. "And the dead don't walk. Climb on."

CHAPTER IV

Speck Steeb's entrance into Oreana was unceremonious. He drew up at the door of the Oreana saloon and fairly fell from his saddle.

Buck Rainey, the sheriff, and "Wheezer" Wilson, his deputy, were crossing the street, and it was to them that Speck blurted his news.

"Git yore breath, boy," advised the sheriff, taking Speck by the arm. "C'mon inside and tell it."

He led Speck inside the Oreana, where he had an interested audience. It did not take Speck long to give them the details.

"Well, whose horse did yuh ride?" asked Wheezer.

They ran outside and inspected the panting horse.

"She's a TJ brand," declared Wheezer. "Belongs to that feller named Swede Harrigan," remarked the livery-stable keeper excitedly. "They took their horses out early this mornin'."

"And one of them fellers shot old Eph Wyatt, eh?" Bunty O'Neil seemed pleased.

"Was the old man dead?" questioned the sheriff.

"Shot through the head," declared Speck. "Blood was runnin' all over him. I took a shot at them two jiggers, and—say, are them the two—one of 'em that busted Bill Wyatt?"

"They're the little vi'lets," stated Snipe Lee, who was the only one of Bill Wyatt's men in town. "I said to Bill——"

"Write it out and mail it to us," snapped the sheriff. "Get yore horses, boys. We'll find out more about this deal. C'mon, Wheezer. Anybody that ain't got guns can get one at my office."

Speck sat down on the saloon steps and rested his head in his hands, realizing that he had incriminated those two men who had befriended him. In the novelty of living at the Diamond W ranch with the old man he had forgotten these two strange cowboys. He wondered dully if they had killed Eph Wyatt, and why. Men were mounting at the hitch-racks, and a few moments later the sheriff and deputy rode out through a narrow alley and joined the others.

Speck got wearily to his feet and went back to the TJ horse. He would go along and show them where the thing had happened, and in some way he might be of assistance to those two strange cowboys. Anyway, he decided that he would not show them where he had found the horses.

He mounted and rode along with the others, who questioned him closely; but Speck was close-mouthed now.

"Yuh say yuh took a shot at 'em?" queried Snipe.

"I took a shot at somebody," qualified Speck. "I never named no names, did I?"

"But yuh saw 'em both, didn't yuh?" asked Bunty.

"I seen two men," stated Speck. "I dunno how they was dressed nor what they looked like."

"And that was one of their horses, eh?"

"I never said it was. My gosh, you fellers talk like I had said who killed Eph Wyatt. I found this horse, thasall."

"You found two horses," corrected the sheriff.

"Did I?" Speck grew indignant. "Who found this horse—me or you?"

"All right, kid," laughed the sheriff. "We ain't askin' yuh no more questions. I reckon this won't be hard to figure out."

"Not if yuh can find out why," said Speck gloomily.

Buck Rainey lifted his head and looked intently at Speck.

"That's about the most intelligent thing I've heard said since the kid told his story. There's usually a reason."

They rode around the point of a hill and down into the big swale, where they drew rein beside the buckboard. One of the horses was on its feet, trying to crop all the grass within reach, but there was no sign of the dead man.

They dismounted and examined the surroundings. Beside the left front wheel of the buckboard was a puddle of blood, and there were streaks of blood on the spokes of the wheel.

"That's danged queer," observed the sheriff. "Kinda looks like the old man had e-vaporated."

They separated and searched both sides of the road, but there was no sign of the corpse One of the men unharnessed the horse and turned it loose.

"Mebbe the old man was only hurt, and went home," suggested one of the men.

"Ain't no boot tracks," objected Wheezer, who had already investigated. "Of course he might 'a' cut across the hills."

"And fought brush all the way?" The sheriff was not in favor of that theory. "Well, he ain't here," he went on. "Ask the kid where he found that horse."

But Speck was rather vague. He studied the country seriously.

"I think I was over there," pointing across the swale. "No, I don't think I was either. Them horses were somewhere over by them cottonwoods, I think. Hanged if I can be sure of anythin'."

"Kinda got buck-fever, eh?" laughed Snipe.

"Put yourself in his place," said the sheriff. "He's just a kid. I'd probably get rattled, too. Well, I dunno what to do. Suppose we ride over to the Diamond W?"

"If he got there, he flew," said Wheezer.

"Flyin' ain't hard, if yuh know how," said the sheriff.

"Well, he didn't know how, that's a cinch," declared Wheezer.

"Didja ever ask him, Wheezer?"

"No-o-o, I never."

"Then don't jump at conclusions. Let's go."

They mounted and rode to the Diamond W, scanning the country closely for any sign of the old man. The dusty road would have showed imprints of boots, if anyone had walked thereon, but there was nothing but the tracks of four-footed animals and wagon-wheels.

The posse rode in at the Diamond W ranch and lost no time in searching the place, but to no avail. It did not take them long to convince themselves that Eph Wyatt had not come home.

"Well, the next thing is to find Sontag and Harrigan," said the sheriff. "If that is one of their horses, and if the kid did find it where he said he did, they ought to know somethin' about this deal."

"I've just been thinkin'," said Wheezer. "Don't the law say that you've got to produce the body before yuh can make out a case of murder against anybody?"

"It sure does," agreed the sheriff.

"And if these two fellers did kill him, and was afraid that they'd get caught—couldn't they hide the body?" went on the deputy.

The sheriff removed his hat and scratched his head thoughtfully. "Wheezer, yore head *is* somethin' besides a hat-rack. Huh!" he said, turning to gaze across the miles of brushy hills. "Yore theory is a dinger, I like the idea fine, but yuh didn't go far enough with it. I could hide a dozen corpses out in them hills. We might arrest 'em on suspicion, feed 'em a week or so and turn 'em loose again."

So they rode back to Oreana, with Speck trailing behind, and found Sad and Swede sitting on the sidewalk in front of the Oreana saloon, talking with two of the sheriff's men, who had been on the lower ranges looking for Bar S cattle.

The posse dismounted before the arrival of Speck, who paled slightly at sight of the two men he had incriminated. Neither Sad nor Swede had paid any attention to the group of riders, but both got to their feet as Speck rode up.

Swede grinned at Speck and looked the horse over.

"I was wonderin' who got my bronc," he said smiling up at the youngster. "Pretty good ridin' horse, ain't he, Speck?"

"Jist fine," replied Speck hoarsely. "The stirrups was too long, that's all."

"Uh-huh. You must 'a' made a hit with Blaze. Ordinarily he don't care for everybody."

"When did yuh lose this horse?" asked the sheriff.

"Today," Swede smiled widely.

"Where?"

"I dunno," Swede scratched his head thoughtfully. "Yuh see, we ain't familiar with this country, sheriff. Me and Sad was taking a little ride through the hills, and we hears somebody bangin' away. Yuh see, we sabe that the deer season ain't open yet; so we opines that it might be a personal matter.

"We're goin' along kinda easy-like, tryin' to see what it means, when a bullet buzzes past my nose. It shore looks like we've horned into somethin'; so we dismounts, leads the horses into a patch of brush, and goes on a hunt for the jigger that shot at us.

"Anyway, we don't find him. We goes back to the horses and finds one of 'em gone. And whoever took my bronc left a good Winchester rifle in its place—kinda like a pack-rat would—so we took the rifle, doubled up on Sad's bronc and came to town to find the sheriff."

The posse shuffled its feet and looked at one another, while Speck heaved a deep sigh of relief.

"That's a pretty good story," observed Snipe Lee, Bill Wyatt's hand.

Swede squinted closely at Snipe, a grin on his lips.

"I thought it was," he said slowly. "Anyway, it'll have to do until we can think of a better one."

The sheriff chewed at the corner of his mustache and wondered what to do next. Swede's story sounded plausible. It tallied with the one Speck had told.

"Mr. Wyatt, the old man, got shot today," volunteered Speck.

"The old man who was goin' to adopt you?" asked Sad.

"Uh-huh!"

"F'r gosh sake! Wasn't killed, was he, Speck?" Sad's surprise seemed genuine.

"We don't know," the sheriff answered the question. "If he was, somebody swiped the corpse."

"Swiped the corpse!" Sad seemed shocked. "What would anybody swipe a corpse for, sheriff?"

"Yuh might as well tell 'em all about it," said Snipe sarcastically. "They prob'ly know more about it than you do."

Sad walked up to Snipe, who began to wish he had kept still, and studied him at close range.

"I don't reckon I've met you," said Sad easily. "What did yuh say yore name was?"

"I never said."

"That's right. You're one of the Box 8 boys, ain'tcha?"

"Yeah, I work there."

"You sabe this range pretty well, don'tcha?"

Snipe licked his lips and squinted at Sad. He wondered what these questions were leading to. Finally he nodded affirmatively.

"Uh-huh," Sad grew thoughtful. "You know quite a lot about cattle and range work, don'tcha?"

"I ort to," said Snipe. "I've been punchin' cows for——"

"Yo're what I'd call an observin' person," interrupted Sad. "Some folks think I'm a mind-reader," Sad shot a glance at Bunty, whose face reddened quickly. "Mebbe I am—who knows? Anyway, I picked you out for this test."

"What in hell do yuh mean?" blurted Snipe nervously.

"In all yore experience on the range—" Sad propounded, the question seriously. "In all of yore experience, mind yuh; did yuh ever know that yuh could tell a cattle rustler by the color of his fingernails?"

Almost before Sad had finished his question Snipe Lee jerked up his right hand and shot a searching glance at his nails. It was a trap which would catch nearly anyone, whether guilty or innocent—an old joke of the cattle country. It is likely that every man present caught himself in the act, except Sad and Swede.

In a flash Snipe Lee realized what he had done, and his hand flashed down to his gun; too late. Sad was into him, cramping his gun arm, making it impossible for Snipe to draw the gun from its holster.

"Leggo me, damn yuh!" snarled Snipe. "You can't pin nothin' like that onto me!"

Sad laughed, gave the arm an extra twist, swinging Snipe almost off his feet, and appropriated Snipe's six-shooter. Then he shoved Snipe aside and stepped back, while the luckless Box 8 man rubbed his aching muscles and cursed witheringly.

"That don't mean nothin'," laughed the sheriff. "I looked at my nails, too."

"So did I," confessed Wheezer.

"Some folks can't take a joke," laughed Sad. "Our friends over there is too thin-minded to fool with. Here's yore gun." He tossed it to Snipe, who caught it in his left hand and shoved it into his holster. His right arm was almost helpless.

"Now," Sad turned to the sheriff, "yuh mind tellin' me what this shootin' scrape was all about? I may be a mind reader, but I can't cover all the territory."

The sheriff did not mind. In fact, he seemed perfectly willing to tell all he knew. Sad and Swede listened patiently, nodding now and then, as though to confirm what Speck had told. The sheriff admitted that the posse had been looking for them.

"I don't blame yuh," said Sad. "It shore looked like we might 'a' had a hand in it."

"Ain't nothin' been proved yet," said Snipe painfully.

"Aw, go look at yore nails!" snapped the sheriff. "You've talked almost too much, Snipe. Go put up the horses, Wheezer. If anybody can prove to me that old Eph Wyatt has been killed, I'll look for his body, but I'm no damned bloodhound."

The posse took their horses back to the hitch-racks, and the sheriff's two cowpunchers drew him aside and imparted the news that they had only been able to round up fifteen head in the lower ranges.

"Didja put 'em in the Bar S pasture?" asked the sheriff.

The cowboys had.

"That's all right," said the sheriff. "Somebody cut the fence and got away with the three hundred and ten head; so they might as well get the other fifteen."

"What do yuh mean?" asked "Slim" Wray, one of the cowboys. He had not heard about the loss. Art Alberts, the other cowboy, listened with open mouth, while the sheriff explained.

"Aw, they must 'a' jist turned 'em loose," said Slim. "We'll round 'em up ag'in, Buck."

"Go to it, Slim," said the sheriff. "I hope yo're right."

Speck sat down on the sidewalk with Sad and Swede, and the sheriff came over to him.

"Kid, you don't have much luck, do yuh?" he said thoughtfully. "I wish I had a home to take yuh to, but I ain't. I've got an extra cot in my office, where yuh can sleep—and Oreana won't see yuh go hungry."

"That's all right," grinned Speck. "I'll git along. Much obliged for the cot, sheriff. Mebbe I can help yuh some way, doin' somethin' around the office. I've got to find my dog before I do anythin' much. He sure rattled his hocks when that shootin' started, and the last I seen of him he was runnin' a sandy on a gopher."

The sheriff laughed and turned toward his office. "Come on, Speck, and I'll show yuh that cot."

"All right," said Speck gladly. He started after the sheriff, but ran back to Sad and Swede.

"I'm sorry I had to steal that horse," he whispered, "but I'm sure glad I yanked instead of squeezed."

He turned and ran after the sheriff, leaving Sad and Swede looking curiously at each other.

"Glad he yanked instead of squeezin'," said Swede blankly. "Now, what do yuh make of that, Sad?"

Sad Sontag laughed softly and looked across the street where Buck Rainey and Speck were at the sheriff's office door.

"He must 'a' meant that rifle, Swede. He flinched on the pull. By golly, that kid sure is a dinger. Yanked on the trigger and pulled the muzzle far enough to the right to miss us. He's got nerve to burn, and by golly"—Sad stopped and reached for his cigarette makings—"he deserves a better deal than he's been gettin'."

"Uh-huh," yawned Swede. "I reckon we better eat. Here comes Bill Wyatt and his man, Friday."

Wyatt and Abe Snow, a tall, dark complexioned cowboy, rode up to the Cactus saloon hitch-rack and dismounted. Snipe Lee met them, talking earnestly, and the three went into the saloon.

"I reckon we better eat," agreed Sad. "Snipe Lee is tellin' 'em all about it, and it won't be sweet news to Bill's ears. I hate to fight on an empty stomach; so we'll fold the old insides around a flock of food before trouble starts."

They walked past the Cactus saloon and up the street to a restaurant, where they proceeded to sit down facing the door and ordered a big meal.

"Well, our alibi sure got past with the sheriff," laughed Swede.

"Sure," Sad laughed joyfully. "You are one of the best liars I ever heard. I'll betcha Snipe Lee is still wonderin' if his nails show that he's a rustler."

"I wonder if he is?" grinned Swede. "He sure took it to heart."

Sad grinned thoughtfully and leaned back in his chair to allow the waiter to place a platter of food before him. The waiter was a pasty-faced, stoop-shouldered person, with a crooked nose and a missing front tooth. Sad looked at the platter and up at the waiter.

"Three eggs apiece, waiter?"

"Yeah." The waiter grinned, exposing the incomplete set of upper teeth. "Thought yuh might be hungry. It won't cost yuh any more than two would."

"Gosh, this is a reg'lar place to eat," grinned Sad. "Do yuh size up yore customers and feed 'em accordin'ly?"

"No-o-o. Them extra eggs are for whippin' Bunty O'Neil."

"Oh, yeah!" Sad looked curiously at the waiter. "Kinda like gettin' a medal for bravery, eh?"

"I dunno about that. See that crooked nose and that missin' tooth? Well, I never thought about kickin' Bunty's shins."

"He got you, did he?"

"He sure did. I was out for fifteen minutes. Never knew what hit me."

"Bunty's sure a character," observed Swede, attacking his ham and eggs.

The waiter spat dryly. "Character, hell; he's a dirty fighter. Somebody will kill him some day, and then he'll wish he'd been square."

"Most all dead men kinda repent," nodded Sad. "What do yuh know about Bill Wyatt?"

The waiter grinned. "You whipped him, too, they tell me. I don't know much about him. Bunty butted Bill, and Bill petted him with the barrel of a gun. They was thick as thieves before that. Bill got Bunty to come down here and buy out the Oreana. Folks used to say that Bill owned an interest in the Oreana, but I don't guess there was any truth in it.

"Bunty poured liquor into poor Jim Steeb and killed him. They tell me that Bunty's got Steeb's notes for a lot of money. Steeb practically lived there at the Oreana. Bunty got him to drinkin' absence. Didja ever see an absence drinker? It shore is awful stuff. Make a man kick his grandmother."

"Did Steeb kick his grandmother?" asked Swede seriously.

"I don't guess he had one."

"Made it kinda bad," observed Swede. "Feller ought to kinda check up on his relation before he starts drinkin' that stuff."

"Must be an awful relief to kick the old lady," said Sad, balancing an egg on his knife-blade. "I never had one. Still, yuh never have everythin' in this life. Can we have some coffee?"

"Yuh sure can. I'll bring yuh in the whole pot."

"We're prominent citizens," grinned Sad, as the waiter hurried away. "If somebody kills us, they'll prob'ly put up a big monument in the middle of the street for us."

"Yeah," reflected Swede seriously, "and they'll carve on it, 'All fools ain't dead yet, but we got two big ones cinched.'"

While Sad and Swede appeased their hunger, Bill Wyatt and his men, Abe Snow and Snipe Lee, stood at the Cactus bar and drank liberally. Snipe had told Bill and Abe all about the affair in no uncertain terms, and bitterly censured the sheriff for not arresting Sad and Swede for murder. Of course, Snipe was still smarting from his encounter with Sad and was inclined to be vindictive.

"He accused me of bein' a rustler," complained Snipe. "Yuh know, he can't git away with a thing like that, Bill."

"He got away with it, didn't he?" demanded Bill. "You talk too much, Snipe. But where do yuh suppose the old man is?"

Snipe shook his head and felt of his twisted arm muscles.

"I can't even start to suppose, Bill. Jist like I said, he wasn't at the buckboard, nor at the ranch. There was the dead horse and the live one. Everthin' was jist like that kid said, except we couldn't find old Eph."

"What did the sheriff think?" asked Bill.

"Well, he didn't know. We had an idea that them two strangers had killed him, but when we couldn't find the body, we didn't know what to think. Wheezer Wilson figured that they had shot the old man and got scared that somebody might find it out; so they hid the body."

"What good would that do?" demanded Bill.

"Yuh got to prove a murder," said Snipe wisely. "If there ain't no corpse yuh can't prove nothin'. A man ain't noways dead until he's proved dead, and yuh can't prove nothin' without yuh can identify the corpse. If they don't never find old Eph, the law won't never figure him to be dead."

"But if he don't never show up, he must be dead," argued Bill.

"He must be," agreed Snipe, "but the law don't look at it like me and you would. Mebbe old Eph wandered off in the brush and died; mebbe somebody took the corpse and hid it."

"But why would they hide it?" Bill poured out a fresh drink and drank it raw. "I don't sabe it, Snipe."

"To protect themselves," explained Snipe. "Jist like I said, the law don't know that anybody got killed yet."

Slim Wray and Art Alberts, the sheriff's two cowhands, came in, so the argument was dropped for a while. Bill invited them to partake of his hospitality, which they accepted with alacrity, and the talk drifted to the fact that the Bar S herd was missing.

"Bunty O'Neil is sure fussin' about that," declared Slim. "If we can't find them cows Bunty won't get the money that's comin' to him. I heard him say that he'd have them cows or somebody would be darned sorry."

"He talks big," grunted Bill Wyatt. "I ain't got no love for that Sontag person, but I'm sure glad he piled Bunty."

"Who are them two fellers, anyway?" asked Abe Snow, squinting through his glass of liquor at the light. "Look like a couple of cow detectives to me, if anybody asks yuh."

"What would they be doin' over here?" demanded Snipe.

"Yuh know they made yuh look at yore fingernails," smiled Slim Wray meaningly. Snipe growled and reached for his glass.

"They ain't got nothin' on me."

"Well, they ain't been here long," grinned Slim.

"What about lookin' at fingernails?" queried Bill.

"Didn't you hear about it? Sontag asked Snipe if he knew that you could tell a cattle rustler by lookin' at his fingernails."

Bill turned his hand sideways and glanced at his nails while Slim snorted with laughter.

"There yuh go!" he chuckled. "That's what Snipe done."

"That's a hell of a joke!" growled Bill, glowering at Slim. "All fingernails are the same color."

"You looked!" choked Slim.

"You don't mean to insinuate that I'm a rustler, do yuh?" Bill grew suddenly belligerent. He shoved away from the bar and glared at Slim.

"Aw, cool off," advised Slim. "Nobody's accusin' yuh, Bill. Yo're jist like Snipe. He got mad, too."

"Well, I'm no rustler, Slim," declared Bill coldly. "I'll accept yore apology, but don't say anythin' like that again. I'm honest, I am."

"Sure, we all know it," agreed Slim. "Let's have another drink."

"I'm hones', too," blurbled Snipe, who was looking owlishly at himself in the back-bar mirror. "Almos' too honesht."

"Almost," said Bill savagely.

It was not often that the Box 8 outfit drank too much liquor, but that night was one time when they threw all reserve to the winds. Whisky seemed to have little effect on Bill Wyatt, except to make him more savage.

But he kept out of the Oreana saloon. Several times he met Sad and Swede during the evening, but avoided direct contact with them.

"Look out for Bill Wyatt," Slim Wray cautioned Sad and Swede.

"What's achin' him tonight?" asked Sad.

"Liquor and a bad disposition. Yuh see, old Eph Wyatt was his uncle."

"Was his uncle?" queried Sad. "Ain't he still his uncle?"

"Well—sure," hesitated Slim. "They're sayin' that the old man is dead, yuh know. I suppose Bill is workin' up a little war medicine for himself. Of course the sheriff don't believe yuh had any hand in shootin' the old man, but the sheriff ain't everybody."

"Much obliged," grinned Sad. "We'll look out for Bill. He prob'ly thinks he owes me somethin'."

"And he'll pay yuh, if he gets a safe chance."

"And he'll get a receipt," said Sad meaningly. "Anyway, I'm sure obliged to yuh, Slim."

But Bill Wyatt was too wise to start trouble with them. For once in his life he decided to let discretion be the better part of valor. He got his men, Snipe and Abe, away from the Cactus bar and walked them up and down the street. They sobered considerably, and Bill outlined his scheme.

"They hid the body of the old man, that's a cinch. Fightin' 'em won't tell us where it's hid; sabe? They've got a room at the Oreana hotel, and them partitions ain't very thick. Here's the scheme. Abe, me and you will see if we can git the room next to them. They'll probably talk enough to let us know a few things. Snipe, you take our horses to the livery-stable, and you stay there. If they decide to leave town, you come a-runnin'; sabe? Leave our horses all saddled, so we won't lose no time.

"And from now on, we don't take no more liquor. We've got to find out a few things. You better go to the stable now, Snipe. Me and Abe will get the room, and find out which room Sontag rented. If we can't get the next one without seemin' to want it, mebbe it's empty and we can take it anyway."

Snipe grumbled profanely, but went to the hitch-rack after the horses. The stable-keeper showed him which stalls to use, asked Snipe if he wanted to take off the saddles, accepted the two-bits per head and went back to his gear-room.

He thought that Snipe went out, which Snipe did not. Later the stable-keeper went out, shut the big doors and went up to the Oreana saloon. Snipe stretched out on the grain-bin and went to sleep. He had a pint of liquor on his hip, which assisted in his departure to the land of dreams.

Sad and Swede were at the Oreana saloon when the stable-keeper ran into them and accepted of their hospitality.

"Kinda quiet tonight," observed Sad.

"Yeah, it is." The stable-keeper squinted around the room. "It always is this early. Mebbe it'll pick up. The Box 8 must figure on makin' a night of it, 'cause they've stabled their horses. It ain't often they do that. Usually leave their broncs at the rack until they're ready to go home."

Sad squinted at himself in the back-bar mirror and wondered why Bill Wyatt and his outfit intended to make a night of it. He drew Swede out of the Oreana and they made the rounds, looking for Bill and his gang, who were not in evidence.

"You think they're layin' for us?" asked Swede.

"I dunno," Sad grinned thoughtfully. "Mebbe they are. Let's look a little further."

They went down the street to the hotel and entered the dingy little office, which was little more than a wide hall, lighted by a hanging lamp. The rooms were all on the second floor. Behind the little counter sat the proprietor, tilted back against the wall, reading a year-old magazine.

"Goin' to bed early, ain't yuh?" he asked.

"It is a little early," agreed Sad.

"Sober, too," observed the proprietor, and laughed at his own wit. "They don't usually go to bed sober on Sat'day night here. Bill Wyatt and Abe Snow got too much under their belts, and bought a room a while ago. They sure must 'a' punished a lot of hooch."

"Yeah, I reckon they did," laughed Sad. "They'll prob'ly snore all night and keep us awake."

"By jing, I never thought about that when I put 'em in number five. That's right beside you fellers. Say," he tilted forward and got to his feet, "I'll git 'em out of there."

"No, don't do that," said Sad quickly. "They're likely asleep right now. Shucks, we don't mind."

"Well, if yuh don't mind. By golly, I never thought about it when I got 'em the room. I'll change, if yuh say so."

"No, that's all right," assured Sad.

They sauntered outside and crossed to the Cactus hitch-rack, where Sad appropriated a lariat rope, which he concealed under his coat. Then they went back to the hotel and climbed up the stairs. Sad cautioned Swede to let him do the work; so both of them staggered visibly down the hall.

Sad carried a narrow loop of rope in his hands, as he blundered drunkenly into the door of number five and quickly slipped the loop around the door-knob.

"Hey!" chuckled Swede drunkenly. "Tha's the wrong door, Sad. We sleep in thish room."

"Tha's right," muttered Sad. "Excuse me, everybody." He staggered across the hall and against the other door, where he quickly drew the rope tight and threw several half-hitches around the other doorknob.

"What's the matter—can'tcha fin' the key-hole, Swede?"

"Thish is wrong key," declared Swede. "Too small, I tell yuh. C'mon."

They went down the hall, reviling the proprietor for giving them the wrong key, which he had not. In fact, they had no key.

"That was a maguey rope," chuckled Sad. "Them things ain't got no stretch in 'em. Bill Wyatt is smart enough to want to know more, which ain't nothin' against him."

"Now, what do we pull off next?" asked Swede, chuckling with laughter.

"Find Snipe Lee. I've got a hunch."

And they faded down the dark street toward the livery-stable, while Bill Wyatt and Abe Snow sat on a bed and waited for them to come back with the right key.

It was a long, long wait.

Finally Bill Wyatt swore disgustedly and decided to go out and see what had become of them, but the door would not open. It would slip past the lock, which proved that it was fastened from the outside, and which proved that Sad and Swede had out-smarted them.

It was dark outside and the two-story drop was too much for Bill to risk, because he was not sure just what might be down there for him to fall into.

"They've roped us in," declared Bill, punctuating his declaration with oaths. "They wasn't drunk, Abe."

But Abe did not care. He had stretched out on the bed again and was snoring blissfully. Bill pried the door open as far as possible with the barrel of his gun, cut a notch with his pocket-knife and managed to tie his knife to the barrel of Abe's gun strongly enough to enable him to cut the rope.

Then he left Abe sleeping audibly and went downstairs, where he accosted the sleepy proprietor.

"Has Sontag and Harrigan come in yet?" he demanded.

"No," replied the proprietor. "They was in here a couple hours ago, but ain't been in since."

"Came upstairs, didn't they?"

"Nope. Said they was afraid you'd keep 'em awake snorin'."

"Oh, yeah!" Bill snorted and went outside.

He made the rounds of the saloons, but could not find Sad and Swede; so he headed for the livery-stable, where he found the stable-man in the gear-room, getting ready for bed.

"Hyah, Bill," greeted the stable-man. "Want yore bronc?"

"No," said Bill shortly. He thought for several moments. Then, "I'm kinda lookin' for Sontag and Harrigan, and I wondered if they went away tonight."

The stable-man picked up his lantern and walked out to the stalls.

"Their horses and saddles are gone," he said. "They must 'a' rode out while I was uptown."

"Uh-huh," Ed squinted reflectively. "Seen anythin' of Snipe Lee?"

"Not since he brought yore horses down here."

"All right." Bill turned and started for the door.

"Say, do yuh want me to grain yore broncs?"

Bill turned at the door, "Yuh might as well."

"More work," grumbled the stable-man, as Bill went out. "I can always think of somethin' that'll make me extra work."

He walked over to the oat-bin, hung up his lantern and unfastened the staple which held down the lid. Swinging up the long lid, he leaned over to scoop up a pail of oats, when Snipe Lee sat up and looked him in the face.

The shock was so great that the stableman dropped the lid on Snipe's unprotected head and stepped back; while from within came the muffled voice of Snipe, demanding to know why in hell everybody was pickin' onto him.

The stable-man lifted the lid and let Snipe get out. He was still half-drunk, dazed and inclined to be indignant.

"Well how did yuh get in there, anyway?"

Snipe scratched his head thoughtfully and looked into the oatbin.

"Mus' 'a' fell in," he said thickly. "How in hell does anybody git into oat-bins, I'd crave to ask yuh?"

"You couldn't fasten the staple," argued the stable-man.

"Thasso? Lemme tell yuh, I'm smart." Snipe rocked on his heels and goggled owlishly at the lantern.

"But yuh couldn't do a thing like that," declared the stable-man. "Yuh could fall into the bin, but I'm danged if yuh could lock the lid from the outside."

"Is thasso? Ha, ha, ha, ha! Is thasso? Well, smarty, couldn't I lock it firs'? Anshwer me that. Couldn't I? I must 'a' done it thataway. Shay," Snipe looked around foolishly, "have you sheen anythin' of Sontag and Harrigan?"

"They left here quite a while ago."

"Oh, my!" Snipe seemed shocked.

"Bill Wyatt was here a while ago, and he asked for you."

"Yeah? Huh! Well, I'm mush obliged. S'-long."

And Snipe went weaving out of the door, while the stableman filled the bucket with oats and fed the three horses. He flung the bucket against the wall, picked up his lantern and went back to his bunk, still wondering how on earth a man could get inside an oatbin and lock himself in from the outside.

CHAPTER V

THE NEXT MORNING SHERIFF Buck Rainey and Wheezer Wilson his assistant went hunting cows. They went past the Bar S, and were agreeably surprised to find most of the last fifteen Bar S cattle in the pasture. They stopped to put up the broken wires, and rode on.

Slim Wray and Art Alberts, the sheriff's punchers, had gone further north, looking for the missing herd. The following day the sheriff was to sell out the Bar S, and he wanted more than fifteen head of cattle.

"Looks like a short chance," observed Wheezer, as they rode further into the hills. "We can't find much except Box 8's and Diamond W's. Old Eph Wyatt must have quite a lot of cows, Buck."

"Y'betcha." The sheriff spat reflectively. "I wonder what did happen to the old man. It don't seem reasonable to think that Sontag and Harrigan had anythin' to do with the shootin'. There ain't no motive."

"We don't know of any," amended Wheezer.

"My gosh, you're gettin' particular. Pretty soon you'll be doin' all your eatin' with a fork, jist to be correct."

"Not 'less they make a kind that don't leak food. There's Bill Wyatt and Snipe Lee."

Wheezer pointed at the opposite hillside, where two riders were coming toward them. They drew rein and waited for the Box 8 boss and his puncher to join them.

"Lookin' for Bar S stock?" asked Bill, after the customary greetings had been exchanged.

"That's about all it amounts to," replied Buck Rainey. "We ain't found none yet."

Bill twisted in his saddle and pointed east. "We seen five or six head over thataway this mornin', and there was fifteen or twenty head out near the Box 8."

"That ain't noways three hundred and ten head," grinned Buck.

Wheezer grinned at Snipe Lee. "What happened to yuh last night, Snipe? I heard Jimmy Logan, the stable-keeper, talkin' about findin' yuh in the oatbin, with the lid locked."

Snipe twisted his face disgustedly.

"I must 'a' been awful drunk. Don't remember a thing about it. Took our broncs to the stable, set down on the oatbin, and don't know a darned thing what happened after that."

"And somebody roped two doors together at the hotel," said Buck. "McKinney showed me the rope. Slim Wray was pretty drunk when he found the lariat half-hitched around his door-knob; so he thought it was a warnin' that somebody had hung to his door. He slept in the barn with a six-gun strapped to his wrist."

"That must 'a' been after we left," said Bill dryly. "Got any track of the old man, Buck?"

"No!" replied the sheriff.

"Uh-huh. I happen to know that Sontag and Harrigan rode out of Oreana about midnight."

"How'd yuh know?"

"Jimmy Logan said they did."

"Thasso?" The sheriff squinted reflectively. "I wonder where they went. I don't sabe that pair, Bill."

"You ain't got nothin' on the rest of us, Buck."

"They're sure full of fun," offered Wheezer.

"They're full of hell!" snorted Bill. "They'll run against a snag, if they don't watch out."

"They ain't so young," observed Wheezer. "'S funny they ain't run agin' it before this."

"This ain't findin' us any Bar S stock," reminded the sheriff. "Want to ride with us, Bill?"

"Yeah, we might as well."

And while Bill and Snipe joined forces with the sheriff, Sad Sontag and Swede Harrigan also rode into the hills, also looking for Bar S stock. They found one of that brand, which they examined closely, noting that the iron had been run on the right shoulder.

"Well, that's one of the three hundred and ten," observed Sad, as they moved on. There were numerous Box 8 cattle scattered along the brushy draws.

"This sale won't be worth attendin'," declared Swede. "By golly, I wish we'd stayed in Sundown."

"I'm havin' a good time," grinned Sad. "You want too much. I wonder what Bill Wyatt and his bunch had to say? I'll betcha Snipe Lee didn't know what happened to him, Swede."

"I'll bet he didn't. Only thing I hope is that somebody let him out of the oatbin before he suffocated."

"Aw, he was all right. That lid was full of cracks. Wyatt was foxy enough to take that adjoinin' room, where they'd have a swell chance to hear us talk, and I'll betcha he cursed the man who invented a maguey rope."

Sad pulled up his horse, as several Box 8 cattle came out of a draw beyond them and moved into an open swale. He studied them for several moments, a half-smile on his face, and then took down his rope.

"Whatcha goin' to do, Sad?" asked Swede.

"Practice a little," grinned Sad, spurring his horse forward and shaking out his loop. Swede swore foolishly, but did not follow him.

The cattle broke into a gallop, heading back toward the ravine, but Sad singled out a rangy, red steer and spurred swiftly in pursuit. The animal twisted along the edge of the shallow ravine, trying to reach the cover of a willow thicket, but the loop sailed true, dropped fair over the horns, and Sad Sontag made his dally around the horn in approved style.

It was all very well done, except that Sad's cinch was far too loose for a roping-stunt, and when the jerk came it yanked the saddle high up over the horse's withers, throwing it sideways, and upsetting the calculations of a well regulated roping horse.

The big steer took a header into the brush, the horse skidded sideways over the edge of the washout, and Sad went out of the saddle, much after the manner of a flying-squirrel hunting for a more favorable location.

The action had hardly taken place before Swede spurred past, his own rope in hand, dismounted almost on the run and proceeded to hog-tie the steer, which had had the shock of its life. Sad's horse regained its feet, kicked a few times, blew the alkali dust from its nostrils and looked back at Sad, who was sitting against the opposite bank, rubbing the alkali out of his eyes.

"You rised something, didn't yuh?" fleered Swede, red of face. "You'll never get no sense, Sad Sontag. Ropin' a steer as big as that one on a loose cinch! I've seen a lot of fools in my time!"

"You hadn't ort to be vain," said Sad painfully. "It's all right for a feller of yore physique to look in a mirror, but he shouldn't brag about it. Didja tie up the little pet?"

"Yeah, I tied it," Swede spat out some alkali viciously. "If I hadn't, that red steer would 'a' made a pet out of you, cowboy."

"Thank yuh kindly, Swede." Sad climbed out, after working his saddle back into place, and walked over to the wheezing steer. It was lying on its right side, glaring its hate from a pair of blood-shot eyes.

Sad squatted on his heels and reached for his cigarette papers, while Swede complained audibly.

"I dunno why yuh done this, Sad. That steer feels the insult awful strong, and I'm goin' to ask *you* to turn it loose. I'm no matador. I'll betcha even money that when yuh take the piggin'-string off that steer, he'll beat yuh to yore bronc."

Sad frowned over his cigarette, and sang mournfully, "O-o-o-oh, Susie Jones was a clingin' vi-i-i-ine, but her father was a pi-i-i-izen o-o-oak."

"Oh, all right," sighed Swede.

Sad got to his feet and walked over to the steer.

"C'mere, Swede, and help me turn him over."

"Do yuh think he's tired, Sad? And after we turn him over, do we have to set him up for a spell?"

"Don't strain yourself," grinned Sad. They completed their turning process, when something unexpected happened.

"Don't move, gents!"

It was the voice of Buck Rainey, the sheriff of Oreana. Sad and Swede whirled quickly to see Buck, Wheezer Wilson, Bill Wyatt and Snipe Lee, standing just a few feet away, guns in hand.

"Keep yore hands where they are," warned the sheriff. "Get their guns, Wheezer."

Wheezer came forward and emptied their holsters, while the two Sundown cowboys looked blankly at each other.

"We been watchin' yuh," said the sheriff easily. "Yuh see, it ain't ethical to hang yore rope on other men's stock in this range, Sontag."

"That's one of my animals, too," said Wyatt angrily.

"I shore apologize," said Sad contritely.

"Apologize!" snorted Bill. "I—guess—you—would!"

"Yuh might at least be gentleman enough to accept it."

"Huh? Say," Bill Wyatt's voice shook with anger, "do yuh think yuh can get away with jist an apology? What kind of a cow-country didja come from, anyway?"

"Pretty fair," said Sad seriously. "'Course it ain't the best in the state, but we kinda like it up there. Lots of nice folks up thataway, Wyatt."

"Yeah, I'll betcha!"

"Got 'em before they had a chance to heat an iron," observed Snipe. The sheriff looked all around and even inspected their saddles. He seemed disappointed not to find anything which they might have used to misbrand an animal. He brought Sad's horse up beside Swede's, and dropped the reins.

"I don't sabe this," he admitted. "What was you fellers tryin' to do, anyway?"

"Jist bein' playful," grinned Swede.

"Yeah, I'll betcha." The sheriff scratched his chin and studied the steer. Wheezer squatted on his heels, holding Sad's gun in one hand, and Swede's in the other.

"Well, I reckon I'll have to take you fellers to town." The sheriff motioned to Snipe Lee. "Let the steer go, Snipe. We've got enough witnesses to this, I reckon."

"Yo're danged right we have!" grunted Bill Wyatt.

Snipe Lee walked over to the steer and loosened the rope. It was not the ethical thing to do, and under any other circumstances, it is doubtful that any of them would have considered turning a range steer loose among unmounted men.

Wheezer had placed the two six-shooters on his lap, holding them between his shirt and chaps, as he manufactured a cigarette.

Snipe yanked off the rope and stepped back, slapping the big red animal across the rump with the coils. The steer heaved to its feet with a deep bellow of rage, whirled with the agility of a deer and lunged straight at Buck Rainey and Bill Wyatt, who were standing close together.

The left horn of the animal caught in one side of Buck's vest, threw him off his feet and he went headlong into the washout, while Wyatt and Wheezer collided, each having a different idea of which way to go, and they went down together.

The steer whirled at the brink of the washout and headed for Snipe Lee, who was waving his rope and yelling unheard advice to everyone. Sad and Swede were not merely spectators. Wheezer had forgotten the fact that he was custodian of the captured artillery, and the guns had barely fallen in the dust when Sad swept them up, whirled and went into his saddle.

Swede was mounted almost as soon, and while the sheriff's posse scrambled for safety and took pot-shots at the infuriated steer, Sad and Swede rode out of gunshot, turning their tear-streaked faces toward a place where they might cry out their mirth in safety.

A forty-five bullet finally took all the fight out of the steer, and the dusty, scratched, bruised and otherwise injured posse managed to get together for a mutual condemnation meeting. Wheezer had lost a tooth in his collision with Wyatt, and he seemed inclined to think that Wyatt had done it with malice aforethought. Snipe Lee had a lump the size of an egg over his right eye, which pained him greatly.

"Blame yourself for that, Snipe," wailed Wheezer. "You hit yourself with that hondo."

"I did not! The steer hit me!"

"You never was within fifty feet of that steer!"

"What did yuh turn it loose for?" demanded Wyatt.

"He told me to," pointing at Buck, who was rubbing his shoulder.

"Ain't you got no sense of your own?" queried Wyatt painfully.

"You ort to listen to nobody but Bill," declared Wheezer sarcastically. "He's yore boss, Snipe—the clumsy danged fool! Yeah, I mean you, Bill! How didja ever expect to dodge a steer, goin' the way you was? If it hadn't been for you, I'd still have them guns and we'd have our prisoners."

"You didn't have them guns when we met," declared Wyatt. "Not by a dang sight, you didn't! An' I'm no clumsy danged fool, either."

"Well, you ain't an active one, that's a cinch. No, and by golly, you ain't no medium one."

"Aw-w-w, don't fight about it," wailed Buck. "Neither one of yuh are acrobats, and yo're both fools. Why didn't yuh watch the prisoners?"

"Why didn't you?" countered Wheezer angrily.

"'Cause I was hangin' to that steer's horn by my vest, that's why. It's a danged good thing that vests don't have sleeves."

"Well, we might as well go back," said Wheezer painfully. He put his right forefinger in his mouth and invited them to inspect the damage within.

"Aw-w-gle ugl nahk umf foot 'n aw-w-gl," he told them distinctly.

"Yawgl nawgl woggle," replied the sheriff seriously.

Wheezer spat painfully. "Think yo're danged smart, don'tcha?"

"Well, I can talk any language you can. Let's go home."

They limped back down the draw to where they had left their horses, mounted and went back toward Oreana.

"What'll you do if them fellers come back to Oreana?" asked Bill Wyatt.

"Yuh don't think they will, do yuh?" asked Buck.

"I said, if they do."

"Oh, yeah." The sheriff was inclined to be sarcastic. "Well, if they do, I don't know what I'll do, Bill. And if they don't, I don't know either; so there yuh are. There wasn't a thing around there that they could use to blot a brand nor change one."

"Then why did they throw that steer?" demanded Bill.

"I dunno, do you? If this askin' questions is some kind of a game, deal me a hand. You seen as much of it as I did."

"Why did they turn that steer over, if they wasn't goin' to get at the brand?" remarked Lee.

The sheriff turned in his saddle and glared at Snipe.

"That'll be about all for this lesson," he said angrily.

"Well, can't we discuss the thing?" asked Bill peevishly.

"Shore yuh can. But don't ask me things. I ain't got no brains, and I'm willin' to admit it. I don't know the why of anythin'. Go ahead and ask Snipe a few questions, if yuh must ask somebody."

"Ask him why he turned that steer loose," suggested Wheezer.

"Or yuh might go and ask the steer," said Buck. "He prob'ly heard 'em say what they was goin' to do with him."

The questions ended right there, and the four men said little more to each other on the way to Oreana. It was rather late in the afternoon when they arrived. The sheriff and Wheezer went to their office, where they rubbed their bruises with liniment and used up their supply of courtplaster.

"This afternoon's work wasn't anythin' to brag about," said Buck meaningly. "I don't reckon that Bill and Snipe will spread the joyous tidin's; so we won't."

"I read about a sheriff that always got his man," said Wheezer. "He jist never made no mistakes. I don't jist remember who the feller was that wrote the book."

"Some feller with considerable imagination," said Buck.

"Yeah, I sh'd say he did," agreed Wheezer. "He'd prob'ly been able to figure out what them two fellers was tryin' to do with that red steer, Buck. Nobody had to ask him questions. Shucks, he up and tells 'em right on the spot.

"I never seen such a feller as this'n was. Deduct things! Whooee! Always knowed jist what to say, too. As I said before, nobody had to ask him any questions. I suppose he could 'a' answered any question without no trouble. And I s'pose he would, too."

Buck squinted at Wheezer, who was innocently examining his mouth in the mirror.

"And nobody asked him any questions, Wheezer?"

"Nossir."

"Well, I wish I could be elected in his county. If yo're tryin' to make me mad—go ahead, pardner. I know just how much I can stand, and you don't."

"Well," grinned Wheezer. "I ain't fool enough to ask yuh when you've got a-plenty."

A few minutes later there entered young Speck Steeb, carrying Boze, the pup, in his arms and smiling triumphantly.

"The gol derned pup found me," he declared.

"Where did he find yuh?" grinned Wheezer.

"In the restaurant garbage can."

"My gosh!" exploded Buck. "What was you doin' in the garbage can, Speck?"

"Well," grinned Speck, "that's where I found Boze."

"Our family is all united," observed Wheezer. "I reckon we'll pick fleas from now on, Buck. What do yuh know, Speck?"

"I know that Bill Wyatt is tellin' folks that Sontag and Harrigan are rustlers. He said they was ropin' his cows, and that they got away from yuh. Is that right?"

"He's tellin' it, is he?" grunted Buck.

"Yeah, and he said that it was time that the cattlemen took the law in their own hands."

Buck and Wheezer looked at each other. Wheezer grinned widely, but Buck was serious. Slim Wray and Art Alberts rode up to the front of the office and dismounted. They were dusty and tired.

"We put twenty-five head in the Bar S pasture," said Slim. "And that's every darned head we could find. We picked most of 'em up near the Box 8, and it kinda looks like they might be a little bunch that got away from that main herd. If that bunch hadn't been stolen, it's a cinch we'd find more, Buck."

"I s'pose," nodded Buck. "It ain't goin' to be much of a sale, but we'll sell what there is."

"Sontag and Harrigan came down here to buy stock, didn't they?"

"That kinda remains to be seen, Slim. They probably won't be at the sale tomorrow."

"I'd like to make a bet on that," said Speck.

Buck laughed at the boy. "You'd like to bet on it, eh? What have yuh got to bet?"

"Well," Speck hesitated and shifted his feet. "I ain't got no money, but I'll bet—I'll bet my dog."

Buck rubbed his chin thoughtfully for a moment.

"No bet, Speck," he said. "Yore hunch is too good. Any old time a kid is willin' to bet his dog, the odds are all agin' the other feller."

Abe Snow had been in town nearly all day, and now he rode back toward the Box 8 with Bill Wyatt and Snipe Lee, who had imbibed much liquor in a short space of time. Abe had been left in town to see if he could hear anything regarding Sontag and Harrison, but it was Wyatt and Lee who had the information.

They rode in at the Box 8, stabled their horses and went to the ranch-house. There was no one there, except the Chinese cook, whose cognomen was One

Bum Lung. He was cooking supper when Bill went into the kitchen to see how long it would be before eating time.

"Two men come heah today," stated One Bum Lung. "I no sabe 'em. One loan ho'se, one bay ho'se."

"Yeah?" Bill scowled thoughtfully. "One roan horse and one bay horse, eh? What did they want?"

"No talk. I seeum on collal fence. Long time set on fence."

"Long time set on fence, eh? Where did they set on the fence?"

"Longside li'l chute, where bland put on. You sabe place?"

"Uh-huh." Bill whirled and went back into the living-room, where Snipe and Abe were arguing over the ownership of an old magazine.

"Sontag and Harrigan were here today," said Bill. "Lung says they sat on the corral fence beside the brandin'-chute."

"The hell they did!" snorted Snipe. "What for?"

"How would I know?" retorted Bill.

"That don't look so good," said Abe seriously. "The sooner we run them jiggers out of the country the better it'll be for us."

"And that's no danged lie," agreed Bill heartily. "If they show up at that sale tomorrow, there'll be somethin' doin'. You fellers keep sober and keep yore eyes open, sabe?"

"Yeah, we'll do that, too," agreed Snipe. "I reckon Bunty will be at the sale, eh?"

Bill laughed shortly. "Yeah, he'll be there. I threw a spoke into his machine, but he don't dare yelp. Keep yore eye on Bunty, too. This Sontag and Harrigan think they're smart, buttin' into things that don't concern 'em."

"Started over that damn dog!" snapped Abe. "If we hadn't tied a can on the kid's dog, these two wouldn't never mixed into it. If it hadn't been for the dog, you and Sontag wouldn't 'a' had a fight. And then the old man wanted to adopt the kid, 'cause the kid didn't like you."

"Glub pile!" called One Bum Lung, and they filed into the kitchen.

CHAPTER VI

"Didja ever read 'Robinson Crusoe'?" asked Sad Sontag, leaning back in a dilapidated chair at the Bar S ranch and looking through a big book, balanced on his knees.

Swede Harrigan squinted through his revolver barrel at the window, decided that it was clean enough, and reached for the oil can.

"Know it by heart," he declared wisely. "It was written on Friday by a man who found tracks in the sand. Where'd yuh get that book, Sad?"

"Found it upstairs. It's probably a book that old man Steeb gave to the kid on Christmas. I ain't read that story for years, and it kinda brings back memories of my childhood."

"Yeah, it must," agreed Swede. "You was eighteen years old before yuh learned to spell yore name."

"Oh, yeah, that's right. Well, it brings back memories of my callow youth. How does that suit yuh?"

"Suits me," Swede shoved the gun into his holster and wiped his hands on his knees. "That danged deputy sheriff shore was careless to let our guns fall in the dust thataway. Say, I wonder what they'll say when we show up at the sale? I dunno whether it'll be just the right thing to do, or not, Sad.

"We don't know how the sheriff feels about it. My gosh, he may be out gunnin' for us right now. He—say, why don'tcha listen to me? You don't seem to care a dang, Sad."

"I was just wonderin'," said Sad thoughtfully. "By golly, it'll be a good way to find out for sure."

"Find out what?"

"What didja say, Swede?"

"Well, now that's sure intelligible," declared Swede. "I suppose yuh found somethin' in that book that'll help yuh out, didn't yuh?"

"Uh-huh—mebbe. When yuh don't know the answer to anythin'—look in the book and see," grinned Sad. "In a couple of hours they'll come out here to hold that sale, and I might read 'em somethin' out of the book."

"I hope Bill Wyatt and his gang shows up," mused Swede. "If the Lord ever did make three danged fools, them are the ones. They're either ignorant, or they've got a lot of nerve."

"They think they're clever," grinned Sad.

"Then this is an awful ignorant settlement. We better get all set before they show up."

And while Sad and Swede got ready to receive them, the delegation rode from Oreana to attend the sale. Several buyers had come from the lower ranges, lured by the chance of buying something cheap.

Bunty O'Neil rode with the sheriff and his assistant, Wheezer. He was in hopes that the sale would bring enough money to pay his notes against the Bar S; but the sheriff assured him that it would not. The ranch itself was not worth over five thousand, and thirty or forty head of cattle would not bring enough more to cover the amount of the notes.

It was doubtful if a buyer could be found for the ranch. The story of the arrest and escape of Sad and Swede had become known, although the steer episode had only been touched upon lightly. Bill Wyatt and his two men rode together, and it seemed that they were unusually quiet of demeanor.

Speck rode with the sheriff, and was still willing to bet his dog that Sad and Swede would attend the sale. Speck had begun to realize that the Bar S was to be sold for debts, and that it no longer would be home to him. Buck Rainey had explained it to him in detail, and a great wrath welled up within Speck against Bunty O'Neil, the man who was indirectly responsible for this loss.

"That shore is dirty work," Speck declared hotly. "Don't I have the worst luck? Lose m' ranch, and then somebody shoots the old man who was goin' to help me out. I hope to gosh that somebody gets paid for all this."

They rode in at the Bar S and dismounted at the big corral near the stable. The sheriff sent Slim Wray and Art Alberts to round up the cattle in the pasture, while the buyers walked around, inspecting the buildings. The sheriff was a busy man, trying to get an opinion on the value of the ranch itself, but none of the cattlemen seemed inclined to make a bid. Bunty sat on the corral fence, gloomy of face, surly of speech. He wanted his money, and he did not care who knew it.

"Close to ten thousand," he wailed, when someone asked him how much the place owed him. "Got the notes right with me. That's the last time anybody will ever hook me for that much."

"Well, where are all the Bar S cattle?" asked Gilroy, a rancher, who owned an outfit on Bitter River. He arrived too late to find out that the cattle had disappeared.

"Stolen," said Wheezer.

"Stolen? How long since they disappeared?"

Wheezer started to explain, but the boys were bringing the herd; so those at the corral separated and helped swing them in through the wide gate.

"Hey!" called Slim. "There's a Box 8 in that bunch."

"Leave him in," yelled the sheriff. "We can cut him out later."

They shut the gate behind the last animal and prepared for the sale. The assemblage sat down on the top-pole of the corral fence and watched the cattle milling around, seeking an exit. The dust clouded up the scene to some extent, but the men were all old dust-eaters and did not mind.

"There's thirty-nine head," declared the sheriff. "It's a mixture of breeds, ages, et cettery. How much am I bid for the bunch?"

"Three hundred and ninety dollars," offered the Bitter River man. The price of ten dollars per head brought a laugh from the crowd.

"Three hundred and ninety-one," bid another.

"Three ninety-one and two-bits."

"Three ninety-two."

"Wait a minute," begged the sheriff. "My gosh, that ain't no way to bid. Them animals would be dirt cheap at thirty per head."

"I'll give twenty dollars per head."

The sheriff turned quickly at the sound of a familiar voice. Sad Sontag was just outside the corral and behind the men on the fence. Bunty O'Neil tried to turn quickly and almost fell off the fence. Swede Harrigan was standing near Sad, hanging on to the neck of a half filled gunny-sack, a grin on his face.

"Well, I'll be damned!" The sheriff seemed justified in making his statement. He climbed over the fence and faced Sad, who merely grinned and asked the sheriff if his bid was high enough to buy the cattle.

"Hello, Mr. Sontag," called Young Speck from his perch.

"Hello, Speck. How's Boze?"

"He's fine. By golly, I'm glad they didn't catch yuh."

Sad laughed and turned to the sheriff. "I hope the old red cow didn't hurt yuh, sheriff," he said.

"Myah!" snorted the sheriff. "You've got yore nerve to come here."

"Not so much. Yuh see, we intended to come to the sale."

"Don't let 'em bluff yuh," said Snipe Lee anxiously.

"Nobody's goin' to bluff me," declared the sheriff.

"Nobody's tryin' to," smiled Sad. "Let's go ahead with the sale."

"Yeah, let's go on with it," agreed Bunty.

For the first time the sheriff noticed that Sad had a big book under his left arm. He squinted closely.

"What's the idea of the book, Sontag?"

"The book of wisdom," grinned Sad. "It might answer a question that's been botherin' me quite a lot. Yuh see, I've been wonderin' who stole them Bar S cattle."

"Are yuh lookin' for the answer in a book?" asked Bill Wyatt sarcastically.

"Mebbe." Sad considered Bill thoughtfully. "Say, we was up to yore place yesterday, after the red steer busted up yore party. You've got quite a place, Wyatt. From the number of Box 8 cattle in the hills, you must be doin' quite well."

Bill Wyatt did not reply, but shot a glance at Snipe and Abe, who were wishing that they were somewhere else.

"Yessir, you seem to be doin' quite well," continued Sad. "You don't brand very deep, do yuh?"

"What do yuh mean?" demanded Bill.

"Just what I said. Beauty may only be skin-deep, but a brand shore ought to go into the epidermis."

"I don't git yore drift." Bill spoke evenly and straightened up slowly. "If this is a sale—let's sell somethin' and have it over."

He climbed down off the fence and leaned against the nearest post. Several more got down, as though tired of their position, and Bunty O'Neil was one of them.

"I made my bid," said Sad. "Is somebody goin' to raise it?"

"Those cattle are worth more than that," declared Bunty.

"Go ahead and bid more," growled Wheezer. "Nobody stoppin' yuh, Bunty."

"I ain't goin' to bid on what already belongs to me."

"Does it belong to yuh?" asked Sad.

"You're damned right it does. I've got the notes to show for it right here." Bunty slapped his pocket. "I've got enough to more than cover the ranch and everythin' on it."

"Lemme see one?" demanded Sad.

"Let yuh see nothin'!"

"I don't believe you've got a note," persisted Sontag.

"Thasso?" Bunty spat dryly. "Well, I have. The sheriff has seen 'em, and so has a lot of other folks."

"Say!" snorted Wyatt. "This is a joke. These men tried to steal a steer from me yesterday, and the sheriff arrested 'em, but they got away. Why don't he arrest 'em again?"

"That's my business!" snapped Buck Rainey uneasily.

"What's the idea, Buck?" asked Gilroy.

"I dunno," Buck shook his head.

"Scared of 'em," fleered Bill Wyatt.

"It was your steer," reminded Wheezer. "Why don't you do somethin', Bill? Are yuh handcuffed?"

"I still think that yuh ought to show them notes, Bunty," said Sad, paying no attention to Bill Wyatt.

"Why?" demanded Bunty.

"I don't believe they're any good, Bunty."

"Yuh don't, eh?" Bunty took an assortment of papers from his inside coat pocket. "Yuh don't think they are, eh? Then take a look at one."

Sad accepted the folded sheet of paper and looked it over. It was a properly constructed ninety day note for twenty-six hundred dollars, and signed by Jim Steeb. Sad opened the book and looked at something on the fly-leaf.

"Was Jim Steeb sober when he signed this note?" he asked.

"As sober as a judge," declared Bunty. "I didn't want any slip in my dealings with him, Sontag. I never let him sign a note when he was drunk. Are yuh satisfied?"

"Nope." Sad looked up from the book and motioned to Speck.

"C'mere, Speck, I want to ask yuh a question."

Speck came willingly enough and Sad held out the book to him.

"Do yuh remember that book, Speck?"

"Sure I do. My dad gave it to me last Christmas."

"Yuh see, gents, he recognizes the book," said Sad. The men nodded. Sad opened it at the fly-leaf. "Was yore dad sober when he wrote that, Speck?"

The boy nodded quickly. "He never was drunk at home, Mr. Sontag."

Sad closed the book, placed it on the ground and held the note out to the sheriff.

"Take a look at that, will yuh sheriff. I'm goin' to ask Bunty to show us the rest of 'em."

"The rest of 'em?" parroted Bunty. "Whatcha mean?"

"The rest of the notes, Bunty," said Sad evenly.

"What for?"

"Because those notes are all signed 'Jim Steeb.'"

"Signed—Why, you damned fool, that was his name!" Bunty hunched forward, reaching inside his coat, as though to comply with Sad's request.

"Yeah, his name was Steeb," said Sad, narrowly watching Bunty. "Anyway, that's the way it's pronounced, Bunty. Yore notes are signed S-t-e-e-b, but on the fly-leaf of that book, it says 'To my little son on Christmas Eve, from his father, and—" Sad hesitated for a moment—"and it's signed James S-t-e-i-b! You dirty coyote, you tried to steal the Bar S, and you probably killed James S-t-e-i-b!"

Bunty's hand flipped from beneath his coat, holding a heavy revolver instead of the package of notes, but Sad suspected that Bunty was wearing a shoulder-holster, and his draw was just enough faster to spoil things entirely for Bunty O'Neil.

Sad's gun spouted lead from his hip, and the bullet yanked Bunty sideways, throwing him to a kneeling position against the corral fence, while the six-shooter flipped away in the dust. His shoulder was broken, but his spirit, after the shock, remained unbroken. He cursed wickedly, but no one cared what he thought. He had admitted his guilt when he drew his gun. Bill Wyatt's eyes grew hard, and he shot a meaning glance at Snipe and Abe.

The sheriff went to Bunty, reached inside his coat and took out the rest of the papers. Bunty cursed him fluently, but the sheriff paid no attention to his profanity. The others crowded around and watched the sheriff compare the signatures on the notes with that in the book. He turned to Speck, a grin on his face.

"Speck, I reckon you get your ranch back. Your dad didn't know how much of a Christmas present he was givin' yuh when he wrote in that book."

"Well, he don't get much, at that," said Bill Wyatt.

"Don't he?" Sad grinned at Bill. "Don't he? C'mere, Swede."

Swede came forward, carrying the gunnysack, which he upended and dumped out a fresh skin. It was the hide of the belligerent red steer. Swede spread it out on the ground for all of them to look upon.

"Remember that critter, sheriff?" asked Sad.

"By God, that's one of my steers!" exclaimed Bill angrily.

"Yeah, it shore is," agreed Wheezer. "That's the one we filled with lead yesterday. I'd remember that red steer anywhere."

"What's the big idea?" demanded the sheriff.

"We went back and skinned it," said Sad casually. "You jiggers were so mad that yuh wouldn't even collect the meat. We all had some nice steaks for supper off that animal."

"You got a lot of nerve!" snorted Bill. "Tried to steal——"

"Don't talk out of turn," advised Sad. "Sheriff, I ask yuh to examine that brand, but before yuh do, I'd like to say that we know where the body of old Eph Wyatt is. He lived long enough to help us figure out who shot him.

"Yuh see, he had only one livin' relative. That livin' relative would naturally inherit the Diamond W when the old man died. But when the old man declared his intentions of adoptin' Speck, it was a cinch that Speck would get the Diamond W; so this lone livin' relative—Don't move, Wyatt! Keep yore hands where they are.

"You shot old Eph Wyatt from ambush. You and Bunty O'Neil had a fallin' out; so you stole all the Bar S cattle you and yore gang could handle, and changed the Bar S to the Box 8. You branded some with an iron, but a lot of 'em were hair-branded in yore brandin' chute. You fool, the floor of that chute looks like the floor of a barber-shop after Saturday's work.

"Look at the brand on that hide! Keep yore hands——"

But Bill Wyatt had no idea of putting up a fight. He whirled around and darted for the corner of the corral, but stopped with a lurch.

Standing between him and the corner and regarding him calmly was old Eph Wyatt. For Bill it was like looking at a ghost; the ghost of the man he had tried to kill. Bill stared at him, turned back and walked unsteadily to the sheriff. It seemed as though Bill Wyatt were finished; as though he were surrendering. But he was not.

Suddenly he grasped the sheriff, whirled him around, grasped him by the back of the shirt and shoved his gun into the sheriff's back.

"Keep back!" he snarled at the crowd, who were all in front of him. "Make one fool move and I'll drill Buck Rainey. Now, Buck, yuh can back up. I'm no quitter."

There was nothing for Buck to do, except follow orders. Bill reached down quickly and secured the sheriff's gun. The two began backing away slowly, while the crowd, afraid to make a move for fear that Bill would make good his threat to kill Buck Rainey, stood and watched them widen the distance. Wheezer and Slim had moved in behind Snipe and Abe and quietly taken their guns before either of the Box 8 boys realized what had been done.

"Look at Bunty O'Neil!" gasped Sad. The wounded gambler had managed to get to his feet and had secured his revolver. No one had bothered to pick it out of the dust, because everyone thought that Bunty was too badly hurt to ever attempt to recover it.

Bunty was humped badly, with his right arm swinging loosely, his face the color of wood-ashes, but he was making unsteadily for the sheriff and Bill Wyatt.

"Go back, you damn fool!" commanded Bill.

Bunty shook his head painfully, gripping the heavy gun in his left hand.

"Damn the sheriff!" grunted Bunty. "His life don't mean nothin' to me; I'm after you, Wyatt. You double-crossed me, you coyote!"

Bill swung the sheriff around toward Bunty. He was afraid to swing further, because it would give the crowd a chance to shoot him in the back.

"Go back, Bunty," warned Bill. "I'll kill yuh if yuh don't stop."

Bunty laughed hollowly, but did not stop. He seemed awkward in his handling of the six-shooter in his left hand, and the swinging muzzle was as much of a menace to Buck Rainey as it was to Bill Wyatt.

Suddenly Bill fired at Bunty, but missed him. The bullet tore a splinter from the corral fence, and a steer bawled painfully.

"Your luck is gone, Bill," said Bunty unsteadily.

"Like hell it has! I'll show yuh who's got the luck."

Wyatt and the sheriff were backing faster now. It was evident that Wyatt was trying to draw far enough away to make a break for the brush. The crowd was powerless to stop him, unless they were willing to take a chance on Wyatt killing Buck Rainey.

Bill fired again at Bunty, and this time he did not miss. Bunty almost went to his knees, but recovered his balance. Bill fired once more, but missed, and the bullet caused the audience to scatter.

Suddenly little Speck Steib darted from the corner of the stable, circling behind Bill and the sheriff.

"Don't yell!" cautioned Sad. "Bill don't see him."

Bill Wyatt did not hear Sad's warning, nor did he realize that the youngster had sprawled in the dirt not more than six feet directly behind him. He was too interested in his own getaway, which seemed more probable every moment. If he could hold them back until he gained the brush, the odds would be in his favor.

Bunty was laughing drunkenly, as he reeled ahead. The sheriff knew that death was behind him, and he was almost as afraid of Bunty's erratic gun muzzle as he was of Bill Wyatt's threats. In fact, he was a trifle more worried about Bunty, because he felt that Bill would not shoot him as long as he obeyed orders.

They had backed almost into Speck now, as Bunty's advance forced them to increase their backward pace. Suddenly Bill Wyatt's heels struck the prostrate body, and the boy's arms wrapped in a tight grip around his boots.

Wyatt cursed viciously, tried to catch his balance, but he had been going too fast. The sheriff backed into him, and they both went down in a heap on top of Speck, while into them, half-falling as he came, fell Bunty O'Neil.

Sad Sontag was running toward them, as Wyatt's heels first struck Speck, and by the time the three men had piled up, Sad was into them, followed by the rest of the crowd, except Wheezer, who was going to be very sure that Snipe Lee and Abe Snow would not escape.

But Sad was not quick enough to prevent Bunty O'Neil from his vengeance. From the midst of the struggle came the muffled thud of a revolver shot, before the crowd could yank them apart.

The sheriff got to his feet unhurt, when they dragged Bunty O'Neil aside; and Speck, covered with dust and blood, crawled from beneath Bill Wyatt, spitting dirt and blinking blindly.

But Bill Wyatt did not get up. The crowd stood around and looked at him and at Bunty O'Neil, who was too far gone to know what it was all about. The sheriff grabbed Speck and hugged him, while Speck dug both fists in his eyes, trying to remove enough dirt to enable him to see what had happened.

Old Eph Wyatt came among them and looked down at his nephew. No one questioned the old man. They just seemed to take it for granted that everything would be explained. Speck blinked at him foolishly, his eyes filled with dust-tears.

"I—I kinda bull-dogged him, didn't I?" asked Speck.

"Boy, yuh shore did," said Buck Rainey. "You done just the right thing at the right time. If there's goin' to be any adoptin' done, I'd like to have a chance at it."

"I reckon I come first," said old Eph Wyatt quickly.

Speck looked at them, a half-grin on his face.

"I'm much obliged to yuh," he said. "I've got to think about it."

"Well, he gets the Bar S all back, don't he?" queried Sad. "It looks to me like you'd have to pick out all them changed brands and turn 'em back to the Bar S."

"Y'betcha," nodded the sheriff. "Speck gets 'em all."

"Snipe Lee says he'd kinda like to talk," stated Wheezer.

"I jist wanted to say," said Snipe, "that me and Abe didn't have nothin' to do with shootin' at the old man. Bill never told us that he did that, but he was awful sore to think that old Eph was goin' to adopt the kid. Bill had an idea of combinin' the Diamond W with the Box 8. I reckon Bill done the shootin', 'cause he rode away that day with a rifle."

"What about the cattle stealin'?" asked Buck Rainey.

"We done it, Buck. When Bill registered that Box 8 brand, he had the idea of stealin' Bar S cattle. It was plumb easy to change the brand to a Box 8. Then Bunty O'Neil came to Oreana. Him and Bill were old friends.

"Bunty pointed out that he had a better scheme to get the Bar S ranch, and he said it would be safer; so we quit pickin' up the Bar S cattle. Bunty and Bill had trouble and kinda busted up. It kinda looked like Bunty was goin' to hog the whole works; so we tried to spoil his game by stealin' all the cattle.

"We branded what we could in the length of time we had, but the bulk of the cattle are back in a box canyon behind the Box 8, where we were goin' to finish the job. Me and Abe plead guilty right here. We never got a cent for our work, and we didn't steal because we expected to be paid—but to help Bill git even with Bunty O'Neil."

"They're both even now," said Sad. "I reckon there ain't much left for anybody to do. The sale is all off, unless Speck wants to sell somethin'."

"I ain't sellin'," grinned Speck. "I reckon I'll raise cows."

They packed the two dead men on their horses and prepared to take them to Oreana. One of the boys opened the corral gate and let the cattle drift. Speck went back and picked up the scattered notes and the big book, which had proved Bunty's duplicity.

"Are you goin' to town with us, Speck?" asked the sheriff.

Speck shook his head quickly. "No, I reckon I'll stay home, Mr. Rainey. I thought mebbe Mr. Sontag and Mr. Harrigan might stay all night with me and kinda help me git started."

"Speck, you've got the whole town of Oreana to help yuh, if yuh need help."

"Mebbe I have now." Speck was wise beyond his years. "These two men helped me when Oreana wouldn't."

Buck rubbed his chin thoughtfully. "That's right, Speck. They shore ruined yuh for bein' an orphan."

The crowd all shook hands with them, and the cavalcade moved back down the road. Old Eph Wyatt was the last to go.

"I'm glad it turned out the way it did," he said. "I lose a son—mebbe. If we could combine the two ranches, it might be a good thing for both of us. I'm gittin' old, and I need a young man around the place."

"I'll be over," said Speck. "Mebbe we might work out a deal."

The old man laughed and rode away. Speck led the way to the porch of the ranch-house, still carrying the book and notes. He sat down and the two cowpunchers sat down on each side of him, while he looked over the papers.

"I can't read much," he confessed sadly. "Yuh see, I never had much chance to go to school. Dad worried a lot about it. He said that education was somethin' I needed pretty bad." He opened the book at the fly-leaf and squinted at the penciled writing.

"What does that say?" he asked.

Sad squinted curiously at the boy and shot a quick glance at Swede.

"It says, 'To my little son on Christmas Eve, from his father, James Steib.'"

"Uh-huh." Speck grew thoughtful as he looked at the notes. "Is my father's name written on these, too?"

"Sure. They forged his name, Speck."

"Yuh mean that they wrote it on without him knowin' it?"

"That's the idea. Yuh see, Bunty knew he was in bad when I showed him the name in the book. I had an idea that he was a crook, but it took a lot of schemin' to prove it."

"Uh-huh." Speck hardly understood. He pointed at the writing on the fly-leaf. "Who wrote that?"

"Well, I—uh—your father must 'a'—" Sad shifted his feet and looked appealingly at Swede, whose eyes widened humorously.

"That's kinda funny," mused Speck. "Yuh see, my dad never knew how to write. He was ashamed of it and never let folks know. That's why he always wanted me to learn."

A short lead-pencil in Sad's pocket seemed to grow warm and he shifted nervously.

"But—but his name was spelled S-t-e-i-b," said Sad. "I seen it on an old letter I found in the house."

"Mebbe," nodded Speck. "Ma could read. After she went away, me and Dad had a hard time. I don't sabe who wrote that stuff in the book, 'cause Dad couldn't."

"Let's figure it was fate, Speck," said Sad softly.

"Who is fate, Mr. Sontag?"

"He's the guy who tied the tin can on Boze."

"Aw, that was Bill Wyatt."

"Yuh can't see fate, Speck."

The kid nodded, got to his feet and walked into the house. Sad tore the flyleaf from the book, wadded up the notes, put them in his pocket and got to his feet.

He and Swede looked at each other and grinned knowingly.

"Will we head for Sundown, or stay a while and see that the kid gets started out right?" asked Sad.

"Mebbe," grinned Swede, "we better leave it to fate."

So fate nodded and they decided to stay.

www.ingramcontent.com/pod-product-compliance
Lightning Source LLC
Chambersburg PA
CBHW011231120626
46549CB00008B/3236